The

Perf

and Ot

Also by Alexander McCall Smith

Akimbo and the Elephants
Akimbo and the Lions
Akimbo and the Crocodile Man
Akimbo and the Snakes

The Five Lost Aunts of Harriet Bean
Harriet Bean and the League of Cheats
The Cowgirl Aunt of Harriet Bean

Max & Maddy and the
Chocolate Money Mystery

Max & Maddy and the
Bursting Balloons Mystery

ALEXANDER McCALL SMITH

The
Perfect Hamburger
and Other Delicious Stories

Illustrated by Laura Rankin

BLOOMSBURY
CHILDREN'S
BOOKS

This collection published in 2007 by Bloomsbury U.S.A. Children's Books
175 Fifth Avenue, New York, NY 10010
Distributed to the trade by Holtzbrinck Publishers

Text copyright © 1982, 1991, 1992, 2007 by Alexander McCall Smith
Illustrations copyright © 2007 by Laura Rankin

THE PERFECT HAMBURGER
First published in Great Britain by Hamish Hamilton Ltd in 1982
Published in Great Britain by Puffin Books in 1994
Text copyright © 1982 by Alexander McCall Smith

THE SPAGHETTI TANGLE
First published in Great Britain by Methuen Children's Books Ltd in 1991
Published in Great Britain by Mammoth, an imprint of
Mandarin Paperbacks, in 1992
Text copyright © 1991 by Alexander McCall Smith

THE DOUGHNUT RING
First published in Great Britain by Hamish Hamilton Ltd in 1992
Published in Great Britain by Puffin Books in 1994
Text copyright © 1992 by Alexander McCall Smith

Library of Congress Cataloging-in-Publication Data
McCall Smith, Alexander.
The perfect hamburger and other delicious stories / by Alexander McCall Smith ;
illustrations by Laura Rankin.—1st U.S. ed.
p.   cm.
Summary: In three separate stories, children help adults solve problems
related to food, first by saving a restaurant from being shut down,
second by untangling a mess in a spaghetti factory, and finally
by selling donuts to raise funds for a stolen car.
ISBN-13: 978-1-59990-134-3 • ISBN-10: 1-59990-134-X (hardcover)
ISBN-13: 978-1-59990-157-2 • ISBN-10: 1-59990-157-9 (paperback)
1. Children's stories, American. [1. Food—Fiction. 2. Helpfulness—Fiction.
3. Conduct of life—Fiction. 4. Short stories.] I. Rankin, Laura, ill. II. Title.
PZ7.M47833755 Per 2007   [Fic]—dc22   2007005888

First U.S. Edition 2007
Typeset by Westchester Book Composition
Printed in the U.S.A. by Quebecor World Fairfield
2 4 6 8 10 9 7 5 3 1 (hardcover)
2 4 6 8 10 9 7 5 3 1 (paperback)

All papers used by Bloomsbury U.S.A. are natural, recyclable products
made from wood grown in well-managed forests. The manufacturing processes
conform to the environmental regulations of the country of origin.

Contents

The
Perfect Hamburger

Contents

Another
Hamburger House

Joe liked hamburgers. He liked hamburgers that were juicy and delicious with one ring of onion on the top and one on the bottom. He liked hamburgers that had just a little ketchup and that were big enough to sink your teeth into, even if you finished up with a stream of juice running down to the end of your chin. In fact, Joe liked almost all hamburgers.

In the town where he lived there was only one hamburger place. This was because it was not a big town and nobody thought there would ever be room for another one. The place was run by an old man called Mr. Borthwick, who had been running it for as long as anyone could remember.

Although everybody liked Mr. Borthwick, the truth was that his hamburger place was not as popular as it used to be. Mr. Borthwick didn't have the high-tech equipment that bigger hamburger places had, so his hamburgers took longer to make and were not as juicy as they should be. Also, it was clear that Mr. Borthwick's place needed new stools, as the old ones looked very shabby. A coat of paint would have transformed the place.

Joe knew there was a problem at Mr. Borthwick's. Fewer and fewer people were buying hamburgers there. Those who did often complained.

"I don't know what's happened to the place," somebody would say. "It used to be so good, but now . . ."

"You're right," somebody else would add. "I had a hamburger there the other day and it was cold by the time it got to me."

Hearing this sort of thing made Joe feel worried. He liked Mr. Borthwick and was sad to think of his hamburger business going downhill. Yet if Mr. Borthwick didn't do something to improve things quickly, he would have no customers left. And if somebody else opened up another hamburger place, well, the old man wouldn't stand a chance against the competition.

And that's exactly what happened. One day Joe noticed a sign going up over a vacant lot in town. It read:

PROPOSED SITE OF
ANOTHER HAMBURGER HOUSE

Joe's heart sank. Hamburger House was a huge company with hamburger places all over the country. Their restaurants were shiny and modern, with white counters and people in neat uniforms working behind them. They produced hamburgers in two minutes, and these hamburgers, it was generally agreed, were fantastic.

Within a few days the builders started working on Hamburger House. Joe watched them lay the foundations, and then pour the concrete. At this rate, he thought, construction would be finished in a couple of weeks. Once the painters arrived and the equipment was installed, Hamburger House would be ready to challenge Mr. Borthwick's.

That evening, Joe went down to Mr. Borthwick's on his bicycle and sat on one of the old stools. The place was deserted. Joe was the only person ordering a hamburger.

As Mr. Borthwick prepared Joe's hamburger, Joe asked him what he felt about the new hamburger place.

"I've heard about it," Mr. Borthwick said. "I suppose most people will go there when it opens."

"But what will you do?" Joe asked. "Will you close down?"

"I hope it won't come to that," Mr. Borthwick replied, flipping Joe's hamburger onto a plate. "I've got nothing else to do. There's nowhere else to go."

A Business Proposal

The new Hamburger House opened its doors exactly one month later. The first day was a grand opening. To get as many people as possible to visit the restaurant, they placed an ad in the newspaper for special, half-priced hamburgers.

Of course this brought half the town out. Hamburger House was opened by the mayor, who made a short speech and cut a piece of ribbon across the doorway. A giant hamburger was awaiting him on the counter. Flashbulbs were popping as reporters and photographers recorded the event for the next day's newspapers. At lunchtime, a long line of people stretched out of the door and along the street, and again in the evening the place was packed with customers.

Everyone agreed that the new restaurant was excellent. There were shiny black and white tiles on the floor, a big white counter, and a kitchen that sparkled with new equipment. While you waited for your order you could see the hamburgers sizzling away on the spotless grills. Then, when your order was passed through to you, there were revolving sauce containers from which you could choose sauces of just about every color and flavor.

Joe went along out of curiosity and had to admit the hamburger he chose was one of the best he'd ever tasted. Everyone else seemed to think so too, and as he walked out he heard somebody say to a friend, "You'd have to be crazy to go to Mr. Borthwick's now."

Joe had been right when he guessed that Mr. Borthwick's days were numbered. Now, even fewer people went to his place. At night you could see Mr. Borthwick sitting alone behind the counter waiting for somebody to come in for a hamburger. But nobody did.

Except Joe. Every now and then he would go down and order a hamburger. Mr. Borthwick was always glad to see Joe, and took a lot of trouble with his hamburger. Then, when Joe was finished, he and Mr. Borthwick would chat about this and that and just about everything.

One evening, Mr. Borthwick said to Joe, "Why not come into the kitchen and make your own hamburger? You can have this one free."

Joe was excited. He went around to the kitchen door. Mr. Borthwick opened it for him and showed Joe around.

"Right," he said. "Now I'll show you how to make a hamburger."

Joe was fascinated. Mr. Borthwick told him what to do and pointed out where things were kept. Then he let him get on with it.

Joe mixed the hamburger meat with a few chopped onions. Then he put the hamburger patty on the grill and watched it sizzle. Mr. Borthwick got out a bun and put the two halves on a plate ready for the burger.

Joe was surprised to discover that what he had made tasted like a hamburger.

"I've done it!" he exclaimed. "I've made a real hamburger."

Mr. Borthwick beamed. "Well done!" he said. "And now that you've finished, you can make one for me."

Joe went down to Mr. Borthwick's two or three times a week after that and was allowed to make his own hamburger. There were hardly any customers—a few people passing through town was the most that they could hope for. Then, one evening, just after he had made a hamburger for himself and one for Mr. Borthwick, the old man suddenly whispered, "Look, we've got a customer."

Joe peered through the kitchen door and saw a man getting out of his car and coming up to the front door. He was a large man dressed in a white suit and he was carrying a small briefcase. Joe thought that he had seen him before, but he could not remember where.

Mr. Borthwick went to the counter to serve him, but the man said he didn't want anything to eat.

"I've come to talk business," he said.

Joe strained to hear what was being said,

12

but the man spoke too quietly. Suddenly he remembered where he had seen this man before: he was the manager of Hamburger House and Joe had seen his photograph in the papers after the opening ceremony. Joe heard the door being closed and then Mr. Borthwick came back into the kitchen and sat down.

"Well, well!" he said, wiping his brow. "What a nerve!"

Joe pretended that he had not been listening to the conversation so that Mr. Borthwick would tell him all about it.

"They want to buy me out," the old man said, "so that they can get their hands on this place, remodel it, and start charging high prices for their burgers!"

"And do you think you'll ever sell?" Joe asked.

Mr. Borthwick snorted angrily. "To that bunch? Never!"

The Perfect Recipe

A few days later when Joe went down to Mr. Borthwick's he decided that he should make special burgers to cheer Mr. Borthwick up, so he rummaged around in Mr. Borthwick's pantry to find some seasoning for the meat.

There were three canisters which had herbs of some sort in them. They did not look as if they had been used in a while, but when Joe sniffed at the contents they seemed to be all right. Taking a pinch of this and a spoonful of that, Joe mixed the herbs with the ground beef and the onions. Then he put the two burgers on the grill and watched them sizzle.

When the hamburgers were ready, Joe put

Mr. Borthwick's on a plate and handed it to him, and then helped himself to his own.

They had each taken a bite when they stopped and looked at each other.

"Joe!" shouted Mr. Borthwick, his mouth still half-full of hamburger. "Joe! What have you done?"

What had Joe done? As he took his second bite, Joe realized the hamburger he had made was unlike any other hamburger he had ever had. It tasted so delicious and it smelled so wonderful that it seemed a pity even to think of eating it. Yet each bite invited another, and then after that another until soon both Joe and Mr. Borthwick had finished and had only their fingers to lick.

"That," Mr. Borthwick said, "was the best hamburger I've had in my life."

Joe knew that this sort of praise from an old hamburger-maker meant that the hamburger must have been every bit as good as he had thought it was. Now all that he had to do was to remember exactly how he had made it. He knew he had taken the spices from three

jars, but would he be able to remember how much of each he had put in?

Mr. Borthwick picked up one of the jars and sniffed at the spices inside. "I think I saw you putting in a spoonful of this," he said.

Joe looked doubtful. He thought he remembered putting in just a pinch of that spice and two spoonfuls of one of the others. Still, he would try as Mr. Borthwick suggested and put in a spoonful.

Soon two hamburgers were sizzling on the grill. They certainly smelled good, but when Joe and Mr. Borthwick tasted them, the flavor just wasn't the same. Disappointed, they put down the new hamburgers and tried again.

This time, Joe put in only a pinch of the first spice and slightly more of the others, but the result was still not what he wanted. He tried again, but still the hamburgers lacked the perfect flavor that had made the other ones so delicious.

Mr. Borthwick shook his head.

"It's getting late," he said, looking at his watch. "We'll just have to try again some other time."

Joe could not get the memory of those mouth-watering hamburgers out of his mind. That night he dreamed that he made them again, and in his sleep he tasted the incredible flavor of the perfect burgers. Unfortunately, the dream did not remind him of how he had made them, and so the next morning the mystery was still unsolved.

Joe racked his brain trying to remember the recipe. He pictured the three spice jars. One was green and had a small picture of a tree on it. Another was brown and had contained crackers before being used for spices. And the third, which was black, had nothing on it at all.

Joe remembered picking up the green jar and sniffing at the spice. Then he remembered putting it down and opening another jar. Now which one was that? Was it the brown one that had contained crackers, or was it the black one? "I think," said Joe to himself, "it was the brown one."

Joe thought it was beginning to come back to him.

"I picked up the brown jar," he whispered,

"and then I put it down next to . . ." He hesitated before going on. "Yes, I put it down next to the black one. And then . . . and then I took just a little pinch from the black jar!" Joe felt a surge of excitement. He had now remembered one important thing: there was only a bit of the contents of the black jar in those delicious hamburgers.

"Now," Joe said. "The next thing I did was pick up a spoon." It was all coming back to him now. In his mind he had a clear picture of what had happened—surely he could make no mistakes. "I picked up a spoon and took a spoonful from the . . . green jar!"

Joe gave a shout. He had figured out exactly what he had done. Still muttering to himself, he found a pencil and a piece of paper and wrote down the recipe. Then, without wasting any time, he rushed down to Mr. Borthwick's with the good news of his discovery.

Mr. Borthwick was as excited as Joe when he heard that Joe had remembered the recipe. Joe quickly mixed the meat and onions and then, under the watchful eye of Mr. Borthwick, he took a pinch of spice from the brown jar and one from the black. Next, taking the top off the green jar with the picture of the tree on it, Joe took out a spoonful.

Together they watched the hamburgers sizzling on the grill. When they were done, Joe put them on the buns and passed one to Mr. Borthwick. Neither of them dared bite into their burgers, so much seemed to be at stake.

The moment Joe sank his teeth into the juicy burger he knew that his memory had not misled him. This was exactly the same flavor as the other day. There was absolutely no mistaking it.

Mr. Borthwick agreed. "You've done it, Joe!" he shouted in triumph. "You've found the perfect hamburger!"

Joe was, of course, delighted. He had been worried that he would never be able to get the mixture just right, but now there seemed to be no doubt about it. He had the recipe for the finest hamburger in the world—the perfect hamburger.

When they had finished eating, Joe examined the spice jars.

"Where did you get them from?" he asked Mr. Borthwick.

The old man smiled. "Oh, they've been here almost since I opened this place. I hardly ever use them."

"What are the spices called?" he asked.

Mr. Borthwick joined him at the table and picked up the black jar. Opening it, he took a sniff.

"That's sage," he said. "It's pretty common. You get it in any supermarket."

Picking up the brown jar, he examined the contents of that.

"And that," he said, "is rosemary. There's no mistaking that smell."

"Where do you get that from?" Joe asked.

"Any grocer," Mr. Borthwick replied as he picked up the third jar, the green one with the picture of the tree on the front.

Mr. Borthwick sniffed at the contents of the green jar and shook his head, puzzled. Tipping the jar, he allowed a small amount of the spice to fall out onto the palm of his hand. This he examined, frowning and murmuring something under his breath.

"What is it?" Joe asked quickly. "What's it called?"

Mr. Borthwick shook his head. "For the life of me, I just don't know," he said. "I can't remember where on earth I got it."

Joe was alarmed. "Doesn't the jar say anything?" he asked. "Can't we get some clue from that?"

Mr. Borthwick looked the jar over. "Nothing at all," he said. "All that's there is a picture of a tree."

"But you must be able to remember where you bought it," Joe pressed.

Mr. Borthwick was flustered. He looked upset. "I'm sorry, Joe," he replied. "When you get to my age, it's hard to remember things. It can't be helped."

Joe felt a twinge of alarm. "If we don't know what it is, how are we going to get any more of it? There's only enough left for a few burgers at most."

Mr. Borthwick nodded. "I know," he said softly.

Because he had been able to remember the recipe by allowing his mind to quietly mull things over, Joe thought that Mr. Borthwick might be able to do the same. "By this time tomorrow he may have remembered," he said to himself.

But Mr. Borthwick hadn't remembered the next day, nor the day after that.

"It's gone," he said sadly. "It's completely gone. I've got no idea at all where I got that spice from."

Joe was not prepared to give up just because Mr. Borthwick could not remember where the spice had come from: perhaps they would be able to figure it out some other way. He thought for a while, and then he made a suggestion.

"Who do you know," he asked, "who knows more about spice than anybody else?"

Mr. Borthwick scratched his head. "Well," he said, "I think the great Cassaroli probably knows more about spices and herbs than anybody else."

"Cassaroli?" Joe asked. "Who's he?"

Mr. Borthwick smiled. "Cassaroli is probably the best Italian chef in the country. He works at the Excelsior Hotel and people come from miles around to taste his dishes. He's very famous."

"Do you know him?" Joe asked eagerly. "Can we go and see him?"

Mr. Borthwick looked doubtful. "I've never actually met him," he admitted, "but I see no reason why we shouldn't go and see him. After all, you and I, we can speak to him chef to chef!"

At the Excelsior

The Excelsior Hotel was at a well-known resort about fifty miles away. When they reached the hotel, Mr. Borthwick parked his car in the parking lot and together they walked around to the back of the building, where Mr. Borthwick said they would find the kitchen entrance. There they were met by a waiter, who asked them rather suspiciously what they wanted.

"We have come," Mr. Borthwick said, "to see Mr. Cassaroli."

The waiter directed them along a passage and there, in front of them, was a wide door with a sign that said, "Kitchen. Entry forbidden."

Mr. Borthwick straightened his tie and smoothed back his hair. Then, turning to wink at Joe, he pushed open the door and the two of them entered.

Joe had never seen such a magnificent kitchen. Stretching out in front of them were what seemed like acres and acres of tables and ovens. Exhaust fans, like great hooded creatures, whirred busily, and steam rose from a dozen different pans. Here and there, standing in front of chopping boards or mixing bowls, men and women dressed all in white were preparing dishes. It was a remarkable sight.

As they entered, everyone suddenly stopped working and stared at them. Then, after a few moments, a man who was as wide as he was tall clapped his hands angrily and everyone returned to work. The man waddled toward Joe and Mr. Borthwick and stood defiantly before them.

"How dare you enter my kitchen!" he shouted. "You must leave immediately!"

And with that he clapped his hands imperiously and began to waddle away.

"Excuse me," Mr. Borthwick called out

after the retreating figure. "But I have come to see Mr. Cassaroli."

The chef turned around. "I am the great Cassaroli," he said impatiently. "What do you want?"

Both Joe and Mr. Borthwick were surprised. They had expected that anybody who called himself "the great Cassaroli" would look more impressive than this.

Mr. Borthwick quickly overcame his surprise and began to explain what it was that he and Joe wanted. "We have heard," he began nervously, "that there is nobody who knows more about spices than you do."

As Mr. Borthwick spoke these words, there was a marked change in Cassaroli's manner. The famous chef relaxed a little and even allowed himself a modest smile.

"Yes," he said quite pleasantly. "That is said."

Mr. Borthwick continued quickly, "And we wondered if you could identify a spice for us. We have it here." Joe passed Mr. Borthwick the green jar and the old man gave it to the chef.

"Let me see, let me see," Cassaroli said impatiently, grabbing the jar from Mr. Borthwick's hands. "This should not be difficult."

The chef opened the lid and poked his nose in to sniff at the spice. He looked for a moment, frowned, and took another sniff. He shook a small quantity of the spice from the jar and examined it. Then saying something to himself in Italian, he put a little on his tongue to taste it.

"Mmm," he said thoughtfully.

Mr. Borthwick looked hopeful. "Can you recognize it?" he asked.

Cassaroli looked embarrassed. "I cannot," he said crossly. "It must be a very rare spice."

"But maestro," pleaded Mr. Borthwick, "surely you have tasted it somewhere before. You must have!"

Cassaroli shook his head regretfully and handed the jar back to Mr. Borthwick. "I am sorry," he said. "But even the great Cassaroli has never tasted this spice."

Mr. Borthwick and Joe must have looked so disappointed at the news that even the great Cassaroli forgot his pride for a moment.

"There is one other possibility," he said quietly. "Eating in this hotel at this very moment is one of the world's great gourmets, a truly great food expert. We will ask him. Perhaps he will tell us."

"Thank you," said Mr. Borthwick. "You see, it is very important to us to be able to find more of this spice."

Mr. Borthwick didn't dare mention hamburgers, because he knew that to the great Cassaroli, hamburgers would be beneath contempt. Such a great chef had probably never even seen a hamburger.

Joe, Mr. Borthwick, and the great Cassaroli left the kitchen and entered the grand dining room of the Excelsior. In front of them stretched table after table with starched white linens and gleaming silver. In the middle of the room a huge chandelier glowed with a hundred points of light.

As the great Cassaroli entered the room, many of the diners looked up from their plates to stare at him. Then, at several tables at the same time, groups of diners rose to their feet and clapped their hands enthusiastically. The chef stopped, bowed, and waved to those who had applauded. Then, together with his two companions, he made his way toward a table in the corner of the room where a tall man in a black suit and bow tie was dining with a woman bedecked with glittering jewels.

As the famous gourmet saw Cassaroli approach, he rose to his feet and made a small bow toward the chef. Then he looked in the direction of Mr. Borthwick and Joe and made a small bow toward them as well.

Cassaroli introduced them to the man and the woman. He was called Mr. Octavius and his friend was called Miss Cadillac.

"We have come to ask your advice," Cassaroli said in an important voice.

Mr. Octavius smiled modestly. "But my dear charming Cassaroli, who am I to advise you?" he said.

Cassaroli spread his hands. "For once I have failed," he said, sounding very upset about it all. "Where one has failed, another may succeed."

Mr. Octavius listened to this gravely and

then he turned his attention to Mr. Borthwick's explanation about the mystery spice. Then, taking the jar and opening it carefully, he inspected the contents. Dipping two long and elegant fingers into the jar, he took out a pinch of the spice and put it on the white tablecloth. From a pocket in his jacket he then extracted a small eyeglass, which he fixed over one eye.

Joe watched Mr. Octavius inspecting the spice. After a minute or so, the gourmet put away the eyeglass and busied himself with placing a tiny bit of the spice on a small silver spoon. Then he closed his eyes and put the spoon into his mouth.

Mr. Octavius opened his eyes and gently withdrew the spoon from his mouth. "I think," he said slowly, "that I may be able to help you."

Joe was sure that Mr. Borthwick's sigh of relief could be heard all over the dining room.

Mr. Octavius raised one hand to silence them. "I cannot be sure," he said. "In fact, I regret that I cannot give a name for this spice."

Of course everyone was disappointed and

Cassaroli was about to protest when Mr. Octavius continued.

"As you know well, Cassaroli," he said, "I have eaten all over the world and dined in France. I have dined up and down Italy, in restaurants in valleys and on the tops of mountains. I have sampled sweet cabbage in Poland and honey fingers in Greece. I have eaten my way across Australia and across South America—in both directions."

Joe listened with fascination as the famous gourmet continued. There was something masterly in the way he spoke, and Joe knew that he was in the presence of a great authority.

"And," said Mr. Octavius, raising a finger into the air, "I have tasted some extremely unusual dishes. In Hong Kong I ate several snakes, all served in sauce. On the islands of China I ate ants, neatly spread on toast. They were delicious. And, of course, I have had so many helpings of bird's nest soup that I can hardly remember them all."

Cassaroli was entranced by this account. To a chef, such a man as Mr. Octavius was worthy of the highest possible admiration.

"But enough of this!" said Mr. Octavius. "To the business at hand!"

Joe hardly dared breathe. Would the famous gourmet give them the clue that would lead to the spice?

"I have tasted this before," Mr. Octavius announced, pointing to the green jar. "I tasted it many years ago. But I have never come across it since."

"Where was it?" Mr. Borthwick urged. "Can you remember?"

Mr. Octavius lowered his voice, as one does when one is about to reveal a secret.

"I am ashamed," he whispered.

Cassaroli leaned forward. "Tell us," he pressed. "We will tell nobody."

Mr. Octavius hesitated. "My only excuse," he said, "was my hunger. I hadn't eaten for eight hours, otherwise I wouldn't have dreamed of going there."

"Going where?" Cassaroli hissed.

Mr. Octavius took a silk handkerchief out of his jacket pocket and dabbed at his forehead. "It was late," he said. "Nobody else was open. I was traveling through that town down the road." He paused, looked guiltily at Cassaroli. "Forgive me, it was many, many years ago. I popped into a hamburger joint!"

"A hamburger!" Cassaroli exclaimed. "You ate a hamburger!"

"I will never do it again," Mr. Octavius pleaded. "But I must admit, it was a very fine hamburger! I can't remember the name of the place. I think it was called Braithwaites or Bentinks—something like that . . . *Borthwick's*! That was it."

An Exciting Discovery

"We're back exactly where we started," Mr. Borthwick said as they drove home. "We're none the wiser."

Joe thought about this for a moment. It had been an incredible coincidence that Mr. Octavius himself, the great gourmet, had, one evening long ago, slipped into Mr. Borthwick's hamburger place. And it had been another coincidence that on that very evening Mr. Borthwick had put a pinch of spice from the green tin into his hamburger.

"I hardly ever used that stuff," Mr. Borthwick remarked. "I can't imagine what I was doing!"

But of course Mr. Borthwick was right

when he said that they were back where they began. A great chef and a great gourmet had both failed to identify the spice. They knew nothing more than they had known when they set out. It was very disappointing.

For the next few weeks nothing much happened. Then, one evening when Joe came by to help Mr. Borthwick paint some shelves, Mr. Borthwick gave him some bad news.

"I don't think we'll bother to work tonight," he said dejectedly.

Joe was surprised. "But we were going to paint those shelves," hc protested. "Why don't we start tonight?"

Mr. Borthwick sat down on his chair. He looked crumpled up, defeated.

"Listen to me, Joe," he said seriously. "We just can't go on. I owe the bank money. The business isn't profitable and now the bank manager says that if I don't pay up in three weeks then that will be that."

"Why has the bank suddenly decided to ask for their money back?" Joe asked.

Mr. Borthwick looked up. "I think I know the reason," he said quietly. "One of their biggest customers is Hamburger House. The manager of Hamburger House and the manager of the bank have become close friends. Need I say more?"

A knot of anger gripped Joe's stomach. Mr. Borthwick's enemies were determined to close him down at all costs.

Joe looked at the old man. The will to fight back seemed to have gone out of him completely. "If anyone is going to save the business," Joe thought, "it will have to be me."

As he lay in bed that night, Joe thought of what he could do. It all seemed hopeless. To pay the bank back, Mr. Borthwick needed money, and he just did not have it. Unless he got it within three weeks, he would have to sell.

If Joe was going to save Mr. Borthwick's business, he'd have to find somebody who would provide the money for Mr. Borthwick to pay back the bank, or he would have to earn it himself. Joe didn't know any wealthy people (nor did Mr. Borthwick), so he decided their only chance was to discover the name of the mystery spice.

"If only we had more of that wonderful magic spice," he thought, "we could make hamburgers that would surprise the world. Nobody would go to the Hamburger House if they could have one of our burgers instead!" Somewhere, someone must know what the strange substance was.

Joe knew that Mr. Borthwick must have bought the spice from somewhere, which meant that there might be a store owner who would recognize it. If it had been bought as long ago as Mr. Borthwick said it had, then the owner would be an old man. And, thought Joe, "as long as he hasn't retired, I might be able to find him."

With all the enthusiasm of a detective on the trail, Joe went through the town phone book, making a list of all the grocers. There were twenty in all, though some of them he knew were large supermarkets. These he crossed off the list right away. That left eleven. Joe visited them one by one, speaking to each store owner and showing him the green jar with the tree picture.

Two or three of the older ones were helpful,

but they couldn't say anything definite. Then, in a little store on the edge of town, Joe found an old grocer who gave him his first clue.

"I *think* I *might* have seen a jar like that," the old man said from behind the counter. "It must have been a long time ago."

Joe urged the old grocer to go on. "Can you remember where you got it from?"

Joe's question was answered by a doubtful look. "I don't think so. It was an awfully long time ago."

The grocer thought for a while. "Just a moment," he said at last. "I happen to have some of my old catalogs. I keep them for memory's sake, you know."

The old man put the jar down on the counter and shuffled off into a back room. After a while he returned, carrying a battered old catalog. In it there were photos of shoes and bundles of string and funny old washing machines with big handles. The grocer flipped to the food section and began to turn the pages very slowly.

"Dried vegetables," he muttered, "pickles, tinned Portuguese sardines, red and green jelly squares, Danish caviar in small and large bottles . . ." He paused. "Spices."

Joe peered at the catalog. The page where the old man had stopped was covered with columns of numbers, but in between the numbers were tiny photographs of jars and tins. The grocer ran a finger down the columns, muttering something to himself.

Suddenly he stopped. "There," he said. "That's it! I knew I'd seen it!"

Joe felt like leaping onto the counter, he was so excited.

"Where is it?" he cried. "Please show me."

"Well," said the grocer, "here's a picture of the jar—it *is* the same one, isn't it?"

Joe looked at the small photograph. Yes. There was no doubt that it was the jar. It was exactly the same shape and on the front a picture was just visble. It was a picture of a tree. Underneath the picture of the jar, neatly printed in tiny lettering, were the words "Mrs. Bailey's Mixture. A taste bud tickler for every occasion."

Joe read this description aloud and looked expectantly at the grocer. For a moment he looked puzzled but then, slowly but unmistakably, a smile of recognition spread over his face.

"Of course!" he said. *"Of course!"*

Joe was bursting to know what the grocer remembered, but he did not want to break the old man's train of thought.

"Well, well," the old man went on.

Joe counted to ten, then blurted out, "Who is Mrs. Bailey?"

"Mrs. Bailey?" came the answer. "She was a famous cook—used to be the best mixer of spices in the whole country. And she lived here, right in this town."

At this news, Joe's heart leaped. All he had to do was find Mrs. Bailey and then Mr. Borthwick's troubles would be over.

"Where is she now?" he asked.

"Heaven, I expect," the grocer replied. "She died many years ago."

Joe felt the disappointment that you feel when you get very close to something you want and then, at the last moment, find it snatched away from you.

"But her daughter still comes in here," the

grocer added. "Every week, without fail. She looks just like her mother, but I hear that she can't tell one spice from another!" The grocer shook his head in disapproval.

To Joe that didn't matter. He was on the right track at last. Fortunately, the grocer was able to tell Joe where Mrs. Bailey's daughter lived. Joe wrote down the address, thanked the grocer for his help, and set off to tell Mr. Borthwick about the progress he had made.

Mr. Borthwick had reconciled himself to the loss of his business and had already begun to pack away some of his old equipment. Now, as he heard Joe's news, he seemed to get new courage for the fight.

"Once we get some more of the spice," Joe explained eagerly, "we can sell hamburgers that will make Hamburger House's hamburgers taste like wet cardboard. Everyone will come to us."

Mr. Borthwick's eyes gleamed: it would be wonderful to have a thriving business once more.

"I'll expand!" he cried enthusiastically. "I'll buy new equipment!"

Joe was thrilled with the change in his friend's mood and urged Mr. Borthwick to write a press release.

"We must put an ad in the newspapers," Joe said.

COMING SOON
BORTHWICK'S TRADITIONAL HAMBURGERS.
HAMBURGERS THE WAY THEY
***USED* TO TASTE!**

Mr. Borthwick nodded approvingly. "You're right, Joe. That's just what we'll say. Everybody thinks things used to taste better. We'll show them that they really did!"

Together the two of them decided there should be a picture of Mr. Borthwick standing over a hamburger, which would be sizzling away on the grill. Underneath would be written in old-fashioned lettering:

Taste the secret recipe of the world's
most famous old-fashioned hamburger!
Try a Borthwick's hamburger today!

Joe and Mr. Borthwick were so pleased with their plans, they celebrated with an old-fashioned hamburger. Joe mixed the mixture, and as he did so, he used the very last bit of spice left in the green jar.

The Perfect Hamburger

Mr. Borthwick and Joe wasted no time in placing their ads: five days later, across the front page of the local papers, were pictures of Mr. Borthwick and the announcement of the impending arrival of the famous old-fashioned burgers.

"I thought Mr. Borthwick was finished," Joe heard somebody say. "But he must have something up his sleeve after all."

"I haven't been there for months," another said. "Maybe I should give these new burgers a try."

This was exactly what Joe and Mr. Borthwick hoped people would say. The only problem was that they had not yet found the supplies of the spice they would need if their hamburgers were to be truly perfect. Joe realized that it might have been better to wait before running the ads in the newspaper. What if they failed to find the spice? Mr. Borthwick would look very foolish.

Without wasting any more time, Joe and Mr. Borthwick set off to find Mrs. Bailey's daughter. It was a long street and they were almost at the end of it when they came to a gate on which the words OLIVE BAILEY had been painted in neat red letters.

Olive Bailey, a thin woman who probably wasn't very interested in food, opened the door. "Come in," she said. "Why are you looking for me?"

For the next five minutes, Mr. Borthwick talked nonstop, explaining to Olive Bailey why they were looking for her mother's spice and why it was so important that they get hold of some of it as soon as possible. When he finished speaking, Olive Bailey sighed and shook her head.

"I'm sorry to disappoint you," she said sympathetically, "but my mother's kitchens were cleared out years ago. I don't have any of the jars she used to use. They all went."

Mr. Borthwick looked down at the floor. Joe noticed that he had the same crumpled look as when he had first announced that the business would have to close. His body sagged. His face was gray.

"Please," Joe said to Olive Bailey. "Isn't there anything you can do?"

Olive Bailey smiled at Joe. "I was going to say that there's something I might be able to do. I still have my mother's notebooks in the attic. I never got around to throwing them out. I think that some of them have recipes in them, but I'm not sure."

Both Joe and Mr. Borthwick jumped to their feet at the same time.

"We would be grateful if you'd let us see them," Mr. Borthwick said.

"We'd take great care of them," Joe added.

Olive Bailey left the two of them for a few minutes to return, looking rather dusty, with several old notebooks.

"Here," she said, handing the books to

Mr. Borthwick. "With any luck you will find what you need in there."

Joe couldn't wait until they got back to Mr. Borthwick's to look through the notebooks. As they drove back, he thumbed through the thick books. Inside, written in spidery hand-writing, was recipe after recipe. Take two pinches of this and three spoonfuls of that: take three apples and cut them into squares: take two potatoes and put them in a pot, and so on.

"There are thousands and thousands of recipes here," Joe complained.

"Just look for one that has 'spice' written at the top," suggested Mr. Borthwick. "That's the one we're after."

"But I can't," Joe said sadly. "None of them has anything written at the top!"

There was only one thing that Joe and Mr. Borthwick could do. They would have to go through the recipes, one by one, choosing those that looked as if they might be for the spice. Then, having done this, they would have to test each of them in turn.

"If only she'd labeled her recipes," Joe wailed as he and Mr. Borthwick measured out ingredients for the fortieth time. "It would have been so much easier for us right now!"

Slowly they worked through the notebooks. As they neared the end, Joe began to despair. As they tried out the last recipe, he was *certain* they would fail. He hardly had the energy to measure the ingredients, and Mr. Borthwick barely bothered to taste the mixture that they had made.

"Any good?" Joe asked as Mr. Borthwick put his tongue into the mixture on the spoon.

For a few seconds Mr. Borthwick said nothing, and then he merely shook his head. "Taste it yourself," he said.

Joe took a little of the mixture and dabbed it on the tip of his tongue. No. That was not it. It was far too peppery.

"That's it, Joe," Mr. Borthwick said wearily. "There's only one thing to do."

"What's that?" Joe asked, dreading the answer.

"I'm going to place a new ad in the newspaper saying that we will be closing next week.

I will thank all my old customers and leave it at that."

He looked around at the familiar grills and battered stools that he had known for so many years. Then he stepped out of the door and was gone.

Joe sat alone in the kitchen. He had done all he could to help Mr. Borthwick, but it had not been enough. Hamburger House had won, and that was all there was to it.

Idly, he picked up one of Mrs. Bailey's notebooks and flipped through the well-thumbed recipes. They had tried all the likely ones and none of them had proved to be the right one. Joe looked at the back cover. It was very dirty from spending its life in a kitchen. Underneath the grime there was some sort of picture. Joe struggled to make out what it was.

For a few moments he hardly dared believe what he saw. Could it really be that? Joe held the book up to the light.

There on the grimy cover of the book, so covered with stains that they had not noticed it, was a picture of a tree. And there was no mistaking it—it was the *same* tree that appeared on the jar of spice. Beneath it Joe could just make out a list of ingredients. It was the recipe for Mrs. Bailey's Mixture!

As Mr. Borthwick was turning in the ad that was to run in the next day's papers, the newspaper clerk answered the telephone. "Yes," he said. "He's right here."

Mr. Borthwick was surprised to hear Joe on the other end of the line. Quietly he listened to Joe's message and then he handed the receiver back to the clerk.

"I want to change this ad," he said firmly. "I want it to read: To be launched tomorrow: Borthwick's Old-Fashioned Hamburger. At last—the *perfect* hamburger!"

The clerk wrote down the wording and Mr. Borthwick rushed back to his hamburger place where Joe was waiting for him.

On the day the perfect hamburger was launched, word spread quickly that something important was happening at Mr. Borthwick's. For the first time in months there were lines of people waiting to be served, and all the beat-up stools were occupied. Everyone who bought a burger agreed: it was the perfect

hamburger. Some people had two, and one customer ate six!

The newspapers sent reporters to inter-
view Mr. Borthwick's customers, and not a
single one had anything but praise for the old-
fashioned hamburgers.

"How would you describe the taste?" one
reporter asked a satisfied customer.

"I'd describe it as . . . Well, it's like . . . No,
that's not quite like it . . . It's just like . . . Oh,
taste it yourself!"

Joe couldn't have been happier. Now that
Mr. Borthwick had so many customers, he
would be able to buy new equipment, have the
walls painted and the stools recovered. Nobody went to Hamburger House anymore, and
it was Hamburger House that now stood
empty at night.

But Joe and Mr. Borthwick had their greatest satisfaction one evening when a car pulled
up outside and out stepped three people.
There, on the pavement, stood none other than
the great Cassaroli and, elegant and beaming,
Mr. Octavius and Miss Cadillac.

The three special visitors ordered a large

hamburger each, which Joe and Mr. Borthwick prepared with extra care. Then, after they had finished eating, they agreed to join Joe and Mr. Borthwick in the kitchen for a celebration.

"I have a small gift for you," the great Cassaroli said. "Here it is."

Mr. Borthwick pushed Joe forward to receive the gift from the great chef. It was a beautiful silver spoon, and on it had been inscribed the words: *To the makers of the perfect hamburger—from the great Cassaroli.*

Mr. Borthwick was so pleased with the great compliment that he had to wipe away a tear of joy that had begun to run down his cheek.

"Maestro," he said, "how can we thank you enough?"

"That's simple," snapped the great Cassaroli, "make me another hamburger!"

The
Spaghetti Tangle

For Lucy

Contents

Aunt Rebecca

There were once two children who had never eaten spaghetti. John and his sister, Nicky, would have loved to eat spaghetti, but they were never even allowed to taste it because of Aunt Rebecca.

John and Nicky had lived with their aunt for as long as they could remember. Their parents were experts on volcanoes, which is one of the most dangerous jobs there is. They had to live in far-off places, waiting for volcanoes to erupt so that they could tell people what to do about it. It was too dangerous a life for children, and so they had reluctantly passed John and Nicky over to Aunt Rebecca.

Aunt Rebecca was a kindhearted person,

in a funny sort of way, and the children liked her—also in a funny sort of way. They knew that, for some reason, she was not very happy with life, but they had never been able to find out exactly why this was.

"I think she's grumpy because she never married the person she wanted to marry," said Nicky one day when Aunt Rebecca had been especially grouchy. Their aunt had once told the children that she had been engaged to somebody but that the wedding had been called off at the last minute. But she had not said any more than that, and the whole thing remained a mystery.

Life with Aunt Rebecca was a little strange. It was not that she was *always* grumpy—she wasn't. But when she wasn't grumpy, she would usually do peculiar things. For instance, they might find Aunt Rebecca in the living room, dancing to music. And it was not the sort of dancing that you would do by yourself; it was as if she were pretending to dance with somebody. She would have her arms held out before her with dreamy look on her face, and she would whirl around the room just as if she were being guided by an invisible partner. This meant that the children were worried about bringing friends back to the house—just in case something embarrassing happened. And for this reason, they had fewer friends than other people. But they enjoyed each other's company enough, and they saw their friends at school.

Aunt Rebecca also had firm ideas about a number of other things, and the most important of these matters was food.

"People eat the most dreadful garbage," she would say. "Look at all that terrible butter and sugar and other unhealthy things they put down their throats."

Aunt Rebecca's idea of a healthy meal was carrot soup followed by raw onions and nuts and washed down with tomato juice. Now this was all very healthy, of course, and tasty too, but if you ate nothing else, then you would begin to want something different.

"Oh, what I wouldn't give for some French fries!" John whispered to his sister as they sat down to their raw onion rings and diced turnip.

"I'd do anything for a piece of chocolate cake!" replied Nicky under her breath. "With a twirl of whipped cream on the top!"

"What was that?" barked Aunt Rebecca, looking sternly at the children. "Did you say something about the onions?"

"No, Aunt," said John in a sad voice. "We said nothing about onions."

"A fine vegetable, the onion," said Aunt Rebecca, peering at the pile of raw onions on her plate. "It's very good for the blood, you know."

"And they make you smell," Nicky murmured.

"What?" snapped Aunt Rebecca. "What was that?"

"I said, And they keep you well," said Nicky timidly.

"Indeed they do," said Aunt Rebecca. "Now eat up, children. There's a nice glass of carrot juice next."

It was difficult for the children not to think about food. Every day, on their way home from school, they would pass by the best restaurant in town. And every time they went past, their noses would catch the delicious smell of cooking.

The children would have loved to eat in the restaurant, but how could they? Then, one Friday, Nicky had an extraordinary stroke of luck.

She had received a letter that morning from an uncle who lived far away but who always sent birthday presents. This year he had forgotten about Nicky's birthday and had written to tell her how sorry he was. And in the letter, to make up for the birthday present, he sent Nicky a crisp new twenty-dollar bill. Nicky had never had so much money before, and she found it difficult to make up her mind what to do with it.

"You could buy a new pen," John suggested, as they walked home from school together.

"I have a pen," Nicky said.

"Or you could buy a game," John continued.

"I don't want one," said Nicky.

They were now just outside the restaurant. From within, there came the delicious smell of food, and they both stopped to sniff the air.

"I could take us to dinner," Nicky said suddenly, her face breaking into a smile.

"Do you really want to?" John said, hardly daring to believe the offer.

"Yes," Nicky said firmly. "Let's go in right now."

And they did.

A Delicious Discovery

"A table for two, please," Nicky said to the waiter as he glided forward to meet them.

"Of course," said the waiter politely. "Would you please come with me?"

They followed him to a table near the window. There he pulled out the chairs and invited them to sit down. Laid out on the table were a crisp white tablecloth, shining silver knives and forks, and sparkling crystal glasses.

With a flourish, the waiter produced the menu.

"I shall be back soon," he said. "I shall take your order then."

Nicky opened the menu and looked at the list of dishes it contained. Many of them were written in French, and she had no idea what they were. Others were easier to understand. She knew what roast beef was, and she had a good idea what chocolate meringue would look like. Then her face fell. John noticed. "What's wrong?" he asked.

"I just saw what it all costs," Nicky whispered. "I don't have nearly enough money."

She passed the menu over to her brother. He turned pale as he read.

"There's nothing here that we can afford," he said. "We'll have to sneak out."

They looked around them. Their table was far from the door, so they would have to walk past everybody else if they were going to leave.

"Come on," John said, beginning to push his chair back. "There's no point in staying."

At that moment, the revolving door into the kitchen opened and out came the waiter. Smiling, he walked through the restaurant to stand at the side of their table.

"Well," he said cheerfully, "have you had enough time to make your choice?"

Nicky gazed down at the tablecloth.

"I'm sorry," she said in a small voice. "We don't have enough money. It all costs too much."

John braced himself for the waiter's anger.

The waiter said nothing for a few moments. Then he leaned forward and whispered, "How much do you have? Show me."

Nicky took the twenty-dollar bill out of her pocket and showed it to him.

"Oh, dear," said the waiter. "I can see that you didn't realize how much restaurants cost." He shook his head. "Oh, dear! Oh, dear!"

"Don't worry," said John. "We'll leave right now. And we're sorry for wasting your time."

"Oh, no you don't," the waiter said. "It's a rule at any good restaurant that nobody leaves hungry. You were my guests the moment you walked through the door, and I won't have my guests be disappointed."

"Do you really mean that?" asked Nicky.

"Of course I do," said the waiter. "Now, what I suggest is that we think of something that doesn't cost as much as the regular dishes on the menu. Then I can get the chef to make it especially for you."

The waiter thought for a moment, then he made his suggestion. "I know!" he said. "What about a good bowl of spaghetti? You could afford that."

Nicky looked at John, who said nothing.

"Well," said the waiter, "you like spaghetti, don't you?"

"No," said Nicky. "I mean, yes. I mean, well, we've never actually eaten spaghetti."

The waiter straightened up in astonishment.

"You've never eaten spaghetti?" he exclaimed. "Do you mean to say that you've never even tasted it?"

"No," said Nicky. "We've never even tasted it. You see, we live with our aunt, and she's the president of the Carrot and Nut League, and—"

The waiter cut her off.

"Let's waste no more time," he said. "Two spaghettis coming up!"

John and Nicky did not have to wait long. Within minutes, the waiter had placed before them two large plates of spaghetti, topped with generous helpings of thick sauce. The mere smell of the mouthwatering dish was almost enough for the children, but the taste, and the texture, and the longness of it . . . well, there are no words lengthy enough to describe all that.

At the end of the meal, with their plates scraped clean, Nicky paid, and the two of them said good-bye to the waiter.

"Come back someday," the waiter said with a smile.

Nicky nodded, but she knew that there was very little chance that they would be able to afford another meal. As for John, he knew that it would probably be a long, long time, if ever, before they tasted spaghetti again.

A Very Special Competition

After that, it was back to carrot juice and raw onion for Nicky and John, with only the memory of that delicious spaghetti to keep them going. They tried to bring up the subject of spaghetti to Aunt Rebecca, but it only upset her.

"Certainly not!" she exploded. "I won't have that stuff in my kitchen. Oh, the mere thought of it!"

"But there's nothing wrong with spaghetti," John pleaded. "It's very healthy."

"But look what people put on it," Aunt Rebecca replied heatedly. "Thick tomato sauce, full of heaven knows what! Oils, spices, grease, meat, and so on. No. Absolutely not."

John gave up, and Nicky didn't even bother to argue with her aunt.

"One day," she said to herself. "One day I will have spaghetti again. I know I will!"

Several weeks later, John was reading a magazine that had come with the newspaper when something caught his eye. There on the page was a brightly colored advertisement with a picture of a large bowl of spaghetti. The sight of the spaghetti made his mouth water as it brought back the memory of that marvelous meal in the restaurant. Then he read on and saw that the company was having competition. He realized that this was their chance.

"Look," he said to Nicky. "We should enter."

Nicky took the ad and read it. It had been put in the magazine by the manufacturers of Pipelli's Spaghetti, and this is what it said:

Spaghetti is best served with sauce, as we all know. But what sauce is the best? Everybody has his or her favorite, so why not send us your recipe? We will choose the one we think is the best, and as a prize, the winner will be invited to lunch with our chairman, Mr. Pipelli, right here in our spaghetti factory. You will see how spaghetti is made and you will even be able to try to make some yourself! So enter now!

Nicky looked at John. "Do you really think we should enter?" she said. "Do you think we'd have a chance?"

"Of course we would," replied John. "Somebody has to win."

"But what about a recipe?" asked Nicky. "I don't have one for sauce."

"I've already thought about that," John said. "Do you remember that sauce we had at the restaurant? We could ask the chef if he would give us the recipe and if we could use it for the competition. It doesn't have to be your own invention—it only has to be your favorite recipe."

Nicky was doubtful, but when John promised that he would do the asking at the restaurant, she agreed. After cutting the entry form out of the magazine, she put it in her pocket.

"What are you doing?" Aunt Rebecca asked sharply, but before Nicky could reply, a pan of parsnips started to boil over in the kitchen, and Aunt Rebecca had to run off to deal with it.

"I can't wait," John whispered. "I have a feeling that we're going to win."

They went to the restaurant the next day. The waiter recognized them and gave them a warm, welcoming smile.

"We're not here to have lunch," said John. "We're here for a recipe."

The waiter was surprised, but when they explained what they had in mind he winked at them and said to wait. A few minutes later, he came out of the kitchen with a piece of paper in his hand.

"The chef didn't mind at all," he said. "In fact, he was flattered by your request. Here's the recipe."

Nicky took the recipe and looked it over. Then they both thanked the waiter and left the restaurant.

"I hope you win," he called out. "And the chef hopes so too. He was very interested in the competition. In fact, he says that he is going to enter one of his other recipes as well. But don't worry—he's sure you have the best one of all!"

Waiting to Win

Nicky filled out the form and sent it to the Pipelli Spaghetti Company. Then the waiting began. The ad had said that the results would be announced within three weeks, and to make sure they didn't miss it, the children pored over the newspaper every day. And every day they were disappointed.

"I don't know why you're suddenly so interested in the news," Aunt Rebecca said. "I'm sure you must be up to no good."

Then, one Friday afternoon, John saw the item he had been waiting for. It was a small notice, tucked away at the corner of a page. *The winner of the Pipelli Spaghetti Competition will be published tomorrow*, it said. *Make sure you don't miss it!*

John and Nicky could hardly wait. When they finally saw the next day's newspaper, they opened it with shaking hands. Sure enough, there on the front page was a large headline that said, *Lucky Winner Chosen!*

"I can't stand to read it," Nicky said. "I'll close my eyes. You read it and tell me if we won."

Nicky closed her eyes. There was silence for a minute.

"Did we win?" she asked. "Tell me!"

She opened her eyes. John was staring gloomily at the page.

"No," he said. "Somebody else won."

He paused. Then, turning sadly to Nicky, he read aloud what was written in the paper: " 'There were hundreds and hundreds of entries in the spaghetti competition. Most of the recipes were very good, although some were not. (Some were very bad.) At last the winner has been chosen, and a letter has been sent to the lucky person.' "

Nicky looked thoughtful. "But it still could be us," she said. "It doesn't say we didn't win. The letter could be on its way to *us*."

John pondered what his sister had said. She could be right. Maybe there *was* a letter in the mail for them. Maybe it would arrive tomorrow, or the day after that.

So the next day they waited for the mail to come. When it finally did, they rushed to pick it up, quickly shuffling through the letters to see if there was anything for them. No. There were one or two bills, a magazine, and several letters from members of the Carrot and Nut League—nothing for them.

It was the same the following day, and the day after that.

"How long do letters take to arrive?" Nicky asked.

"I'm not sure," replied John. "Two or three days. Maybe more."

He knew, though, that there was now no chance that they had won, and when nothing arrived in the mail the next day, he told Nicky that there was no point in hoping any longer that they could have won.

It was bitterly disappointing. They had known that there would be hundreds of people entering the competition, and they had known in their heart of hearts that it was very difficult to win a competition like that, and yet it seemed to them that they must have come so close.

"Never mind," said John, trying to sound cheerful. "Whoever did win will be very happy to hear the news."

After that, they did not talk about the competition anymore. They tried to forget about spaghetti, and to give up all thought of ever eating it again. They also tried to avoid the restaurant. They now crossed the street before they reached it, so that they would not be forced to breathe in the delicious smells or see the diners at their tables. Then, a few days later, as they were walking past on the other side of the street, they heard a shout.

"Hello there!" cried a voice. "Hello, you two!"

John spun around. There, standing in the doorway of the restaurant and beckoning to them from across the street, was their friend the waiter. "I want to speak to you," he shouted. Reluctantly, John and Nicky crossed the street to talk to the waiter.

"Where have you been?" he asked. "I've been on the lookout for you."

"We've been going home a different way," explained John, without telling him why.

"I see," said the waiter. "Anyway, the important thing is that I found you."

The waiter brought them into the doorway.

"I've got amazing news for you," he confided. "The chef won the spaghetti competition. Isn't that wonderful?"

John glanced at Nicky. So the chef was the lucky person. If only he had given them the recipe he used, and kept the one he gave to them!

"Aren't you pleased?" asked the waiter.

"Of course," said John bravely. "Please tell him we're very happy for him."

The waiter laughed. "Happy for yourselves, more likely. He can't go."

John and Nicky looked puzzled.

"He can't visit the spaghetti factory," said the waiter. "He's too busy. And so he wants you two to have his prize. He's been in touch with Mr. Pipelli, who says that it's perfectly all right with him. All you have to do is arrange a time."

John clapped his hands together with delight. He could scarcely believe their good luck. They had resigned themselves to losing the competition, and now it was just as if they had won. He was already beginning to imagine what the factory would be like and what he would say to Mr. Pipelli. And Nicky, although still astonished by their sudden stroke of good fortune, was thinking the exact same thing.

A Welcome from Mr. Pipelli

Aunt Rebecca was not at all pleased.

"A spaghetti factory!" she exploded. "Did you say a SPAGHETTI factory?"

"Yes," said John. "Mr. Pipelli's spaghetti factory."

"You can't go," she said. "I won't allow it."

"But why not?" Nicky pleaded. "There's nothing wrong with spaghetti."

"We've already discussed that," said Aunt Rebecca, "and you know my views. No. And that's all there is to it."

John thought quickly.

"It is rude to turn down an invitation, isn't it?" he asked. He knew very well that Aunt Rebecca was particular about manners.

"Of course it is," snapped his aunt. "It's very rude, unless you have a good reason."

"Well," said John, "Mr. Pipelli invited us to have lunch with him in his factory. Wouldn't it be rude to say no?"

Aunt Rebecca was cornered. Eventually, after a lot more grumbling, she had to accept that it would be impolite for John and Nicky not to go, and permission was given.

"Way to go!" Nicky whispered to her brother. "I can almost smell the spaghetti already!"

"What was that?" asked Aunt Rebecca suspiciously. "What did you say?"

But, from the kitchen, there was a squeak from the pressure cooker, and Aunt Rebecca had to run off to attend to a pot of fresh seaweed.

On the day of the visit, John and Nicky were ready before the spaghetti factory car arrived. The driver settled them in their seats, and they began the long journey to the factory.

"You'll like Mr. Pipelli," the driver said.

"Everybody likes him the minute they meet him. You just wait and see."

They drove for an hour or so before they arrived. It was a very large factory—much bigger than either of them had imagined—and over the front gate there was a large sign made out of metal letters that read

PIPELLI'S SPAGHETTI— THE KING OF SPAGHETTIS

The car swept into the driveway and came to a halt outside the main office. Ushered into the entrance hall by the driver, the two visitors were shown to a door that said, quite simply, The Boss.

"Go ahead," said the driver. "Knock."

And Nicky did.

The door flew open the second Nicky's knuckle hit the wood. There before them stood a stout man in a checkered suit. He had curly black hair, sparkling eyes, and a smile that seemed to split his face in two.

"Well, well," he said. "My two guests! Please come in!"

John and Nicky entered the room cautiously. It was even more splendid than they had imagined. On the walls were large paintings of Italy, framed in heavy gold frames. On the mantelpiece, above the marble fireplace, there were cups and trophies, and at the far end was a huge wooden desk, on which stood a large gold pen stand.

"Yes," said Mr. Pipelli, as if reading their thoughts. "It *is* a splendid room, and I have indeed made a great deal of money from spaghetti."

"I didn't mean to starc," John said apologetically. "It's just that I've never seen . . ."

"But you are here to stare," Mr. Pipelli protested. "That's why I invited you. Today you may stare and stare as much as you want, and nobody will think it the slightest bit strange"

The driver had been right. Both John and Nicky liked Mr. Pipelli immediately. Whenever he spoke he smiled, and when he wasn't speaking, his eyes twinkled with merriment. He was just the kind of person who would run a competition like this, and he was just the kind of person who would make sure that the winners had fun.

"Well," said Mr. Pipelli, rubbing his hands together. "Let's go and take a look at the factory. I've been in the spaghetti business for twenty years, you know, and I feel as excited by what goes on here now as I did the day I started. So let's not wait anymore! Let's go and take a look at how spaghetti is made!"

They walked out of Mr. Pipelli's office and made their way along a passageway that led into the heart of the factory. At the end of the passageway there was a door, which Mr. Pipelli opened with a flourish.

"In this very room," he said, his voice lowered in awe, "we see the beginnings of spaghetti."

John and Nicky craned their necks to see behind Mr. Pipelli. They were standing in the entrance to a large room in the center of which stood a gigantic mound of flour. From this mound, people in white overalls were using large shovels to pour the flour into huge metal mixers. As the flour was shoveled in, white clouds rose like steam, making the faces of the workers seem as pale as if they had just seen ghosts.

"A dusty business at this stage," remarked Mr. Pipelli, taking out a large silk handkerchief that he used to remove the fine layer of flour that had already settled on the front of his suit.

John and Nicky followed the spaghetti manufacturer as he led them across to the mixing machines. At the side of each bowl, there was a woman with a watering can. As each shovelful of flour was put into the bowl, she tipped her can over the edge and poured in a stream of thick, greenish liquid.

"Olive oil," explained Mr. Pipelli. "It's very important in the making of spaghetti. And these ladies know exactly how much olive oil to put in each bowl. They all come from the same part of Italy—every one of them—where everybody, absolutely everybody, knows all there is to know about olive oil!"

John looked at the woman next to the bowl, who smiled and winked at him, and before he knew what was happening, she tossed back her head, opened her mouth, and poured a stream of olive oil right down her throat!

John looked shocked, but Mr. Pipelli just laughed.

"Don't worry about that," he said. "They live on olive oil. There's nothing they like better."

He nodded to the woman as they began to move on.

"Thank you, Olive," he said. "And take the rest of the day off, if you want!"

As they walked on, Mr. Pipelli turned to the children and whispered, "She won't take the day off. She loves her job so much that she'll want to stay. This is a very happy factory, you see!"

Things Go Wrong

"Next," said Mr. Pipelli as they prepared to leave the room, "we will see what happens to the dough. This is the really exciting part!"

Wondering what they were going to see next, John and Nicky followed their host through a door into another large room. This room was much noisier, since it was filled by a large machine, which was shuddering and shaking and making a strange squelchy sound.

"This," said Mr. Pipelli proudly, "is the actual spaghetti-making machine! This is the very heart of the factory."

John and Nicky gazed at the giant machine. At one end, there was an open bowl, almost the size of a swimming pool, where the dough that had been mixed next door was being loaded in great, sticky globules. From there, a number of thick pipes led into the machine itself, one side of which was covered with a variety of dials and levers. Then, at the far end of the machine, more people in white uniforms were bustling around with strands of finished spaghetti in their hands like bundles of wool.

"This is the spaghetti spinner," explained Mr. Pipelli proudly. "It is, in fact, the most advanced and expensive spaghetti spinner in the world. Not only can it make spaghetti, it can also make macaroni, cannelloni, tagliatelle, and every other shape of pasta you could dream of!"

Mr. Pipelli's expression had become dreamy.

"Just the names of all the pastas make my mouth water," he said. "Just think of them! *Capellini! Vermicelli! Nastrini! Farfallette!*"

He closed his eyes in ecstasy, but soon remembered that he had visitors and came back to Earth. With a look of pride, he pointed to the other side of the room.

"And that's the finished product being hung

out to dry," he said. "That's only a week's worth of spaghetti—enough to supply an entire city for at least a year!"

John and Nicky gazed at the towering white racks on which the spaghetti had been hung to dry. "You could get lost in that," John thought. "And if you did, it would be like being in a spaghetti forest."

Mr. Pipelli made his way toward the machine, beckoning the children to follow him.

"These dials control the shape," he said, pointing to a line of buttons and wheels along the side of the machine.

He turned and whispered in Nicky's ear.

"Have you ever seen twisty spaghetti?" he asked.

Nicky shook her head.

"Then watch," said Mr. Pipelli, fiddling with one of the dials.

As the dial turned, the noise inside the machine seemed to change briefly, and within a few seconds the most amazing twisty spaghetti began to emerge at the other end.

Mr. Pipelli turned to John, beaming with pride.

"I'm the only person in the world who makes that," he said. "Now, what about you? Would you like to try a special shape?"

John reached for the dial and began to turn it gingerly.

"A little bit more to the left," prompted Mr. Pipelli. "Now to the right."

Nicky watched with fascination as the machine began to respond to her brother's instructions. "It's round!" she cried out. "Round spaghetti!"

Mr. Pipelli looked over at the place where the spaghetti was emerging.

"Well!" he exclaimed. "What an interesting shape. Maybe we'll make more of that."

John craned his neck to see the results of his adjustment. The round spaghetti was definitely very interesting, and tasty-looking too, but it might be a little bit too short.

"Can I make it longer?" he asked.

"Anything you wish," said Mr. Pipelli. "Just pull that lever over there."

John gave the lever a tug.

"Not so far!" shouted Mr. Pipelli, but it was

too late. The machine gave a shudder and started to whine. Almost immediately, from the other end, immensely long strands of spaghetti began to shoot out. In fact, they were so long that they seemed to have no end at all.

"Cable spaghetti!" moaned Mr. Pipelli, rushing around and throwing his hands in the air. "Exactly what every spaghetti manufacturer dreads more than anything else!"

It took Mr. Pipelli a minute or two to recover himself. During that time, the machine continued to spew out the strands of endless spaghetti. At the other end, the spaghetti workers frantically tried to pick up the growing mounds of spaghetti strands, but no sooner did they manage to compile them than the machine produced more than they had taken away. It was a hopeless task.

Then, when at last he began to calm down, Mr. Pipelli managed to find the switch that turned off the machine. With a last heave and gurgle, the giant spaghetti-making device squeezed out the last few feet of spaghetti and became silent.

Mr. Pipelli mopped his brow.

"Don't worry," he said to John. "That wasn't your fault. This machine's been malfunctioning for a few months. It was bound to do that sooner or later."

John was relieved to hear this. He had been sure it was all his fault.

"We'll have to try and deal with all that spaghetti," said Mr. Pipelli. "Then I intend to do something about fixing this machine."

Mr. Pipelli now took John and Nicky to stand beside the vast mountain of spaghetti.

"It's going to be difficult," he said despondently. "We'll have to find the ends of the strands—then we'll have to roll them all up. That's the only way to do it."

John and Nicky looked at the spaghetti. It seemed like an impossible task to sort out the muddle of strands, and yet, as John watched, he saw what looked like an end. Cautiously he reached down and picked it up.

"Well done!" said Mr. Pipelli. "Now just pull on it."

John did as he was told and gradually

pulled out a long strand of spaghetti. It seemed to go on forever, and soon he was standing at the other end of the room, linked to the pile of spaghetti by a long, slithery strand.

While this was happening, Nicky had spotted another end, which she grabbed and began to pull out. Soon she was standing by John's side while Mr. Pipelli went to a storeroom to look for something to wind it around. After a few minutes he came back, carrying an empty barrel. Then, closely supervised by Mr. Pipelli, the children began the slippery task of winding the still wet spaghetti onto the barrel. It was slow work, since the spaghetti kept getting twisted and knotted up, but at last it was finished and the mountain of spaghetti began to look much smaller.

"We should let the spaghetti workers do the rest," said Mr. Pipelli, who was beginning to look much more cheerful. "Now, let's take a look at this machine. Do either of you know anything about machinery?"

John and Nicky shook their heads. They could put the chain back on a bicycle—but you would have to know much more than that to be able to fix something as complicated as a spaghetti-making machine.

Mr. Pipelli looked slightly disappointed.

"Oh, dear," he said. "I don't know very much about it myself. Still, we can give it a try!"

Tangled Up

John and Nicky watched quietly as Mr. Pipelli picked up a screwdriver and began to unscrew a metal plate on the side of the machine.

"This is the inspection hatch," he explained cheerfully. "It will allow us to get inside."

John looked doubtfully at Nicky and gulped. What would be inside that great, gleaming machine? And what could they possibly do once they were inside it? Was Mr. Pipelli sure that it was turned off completely?

Mr. Pipelli unscrewed the last screw and put the screwdriver down. Then, carefully holding the edges of the plate, he took it off and laid it down on the floor.

John and Nicky peered through the hatch.

"It's very dark inside," ventured John. "Maybe we should call a mechanic. He might know where everything is."

Mr. Pipelli chuckled. "Why go to all that trouble and expense?" he said breezily. "Most machines are very simple once you work out what's what. And as for the darkness, there's a flashlight here. So let's go in."

Mr. Pipelli led the way, followed by Nicky. John brought up the rear.

"I'm scared," whispered Nicky. "What if somebody turns the machine on while we're in here?"

John did not try to answer her question. Yet there was no doubt in his mind that they would be in very serious trouble if that happened. All around them were rollers, sifters, crushers, and squeezers. The squeezers looked particularly dangerous, and John thought that anybody who got caught in one of those would have a very good chance of looking like a piece of spaghetti when they eventually got out.

"There's no need to worry about that," said

Mr. Pipelli jovially. "It's impossible to turn the machine on when the inspection hatch is open. Now we have to locate the part that controls the length. Can anybody see it?"

John looked up, but at that precise moment a large blob of unsqueezed spaghetti dough fell down the back of his neck.

"Perhaps we should be wearing overalls," said Mr. Pipelli, noticing what had happened. "Still, one can't expect to visit a spaghetti factory and not have a little bit of spaghetti dough fall on them!"

Mr. Pipelli moved his flashlight around him. Suddenly he let out a cry of triumph.

"That's it," he said. "That's where the problem is."

The children looked at the place where the beam of light was resting. High up at the top of the machine, the spaghetti had become hopelessly tangled. It was like a giant ball of knitting that had gone terribly wrong.

Mr. Pipelli passed the flashlight to John to hold while he tried to pull down the tangle, but try as he might, he could not reach high enough. After he had failed three times, he stood back and scratched his head.

"I know what we'll do," he said after a while. "You climb onto my shoulders, John, and we'll do it that way."

Nicky held the flashlight while John clambered onto Mr. Pipelli's shoulders. Then, as Mr. Pipelli moved into position, John began to tug at the mess of spaghetti.

It was not easy work. The spaghetti was sticky and had wound itself around and around in a maze of loops and knots. John tugged and pulled, only pausing to wipe strands of spaghetti off his face. And all the time, he heard Mr. Pipelli huffing and puffing beneath him, trying to keep him in the right position. Then, just as he had pulled off the last strand, Mr. Pipelli's legs gave out from underneath him, and John found himself tumbling down, closely followed by the great ball of spaghetti that he had just dislodged.

The spaghetti was soft, of course, which was a good thing, but when John got up, he was covered in it from head to toe.

"I'm very sorry," said Mr. Pipelli, still sounding very cheerful nonetheless. "But at least we fixed the machine. I'm sure it'll work now!"

"But what about me?" John mumbled from somewhere within the tangle of spaghetti. "I'm afraid I'm all tied up."

Mr. Pipelli pointed the flashlight at John.

"I see," he said. "Well, maybe we should do something about you. I'll just start pulling on this piece here . . ."

Mr. Pipelli grabbed a strand of spaghetti and began to tug. As he did, John felt the spaghetti slithering around him, like the coils of an impossibly long snake.

"That's it!" said Mr. Pipelli enthusiastically. "It's coming off nicely."

Mr. Pipelli spoke too soon. Although the spaghetti had begun to move, it had also begun to tighten.

"Please stop," John called out. "It's tying me up so that I can't move."

Mr. Pipelli shook his head. "We have to get you out of here somehow," he said. "Then we can have a better look at the problem."

Helped by Nicky, Mr. Pipelli managed to

half roll, half push John out of the hatch and back into the factory. The spaghetti workers stood around, gazing at John, scratching their heads.

"Can anybody think of a way to get him out of there?" asked Mr. Pipelli. "If we pull at the spaghetti, it seems to just get worse."

The spaghetti workers whispered among themselves. They had seen all kinds of things happen in the spaghetti factory. They remembered the day when Mr. Pipelli dropped his hat into the spaghetti machine and watched helplessly as it came out the other end in long strands of material. They all remembered it very well and still talked about it whenever they saw their employer wearing anything on his head. In fact, one of the spaghetti workers had named her new baby Cappello, which means "hat" in Italian—just to remind her of that marvelous incident. Yes, they had seen many strange things, but never anything quite as strange as this.

As they were standing around, wondering how they could possibly get John out of the tangle, one of the women suddenly stepped forward and whispered something in Mr. Pipelli's ear. It was Olive.

Mr. Pipelli listened gravely, stroked his chin, and then nodded.

"That just might work, Olive," he said. "You go and grab the—you know what I mean—and we'll try."

Nicky tugged at Mr. Pipelli's sleeve.

"What are you going to do?" she asked timidly. "You're not going to hurt him, are you? Aunt Rebecca will be furious if you do."

Mr. Pipelli patted her gently on the shoulder.

"Of course not," he said reassuringly. Then, whispering, he explained, "Olive suggested that we"—his eyes glistened with mischief—"pour olive oil all over him. That way he'll be slippery enough to wriggle his way out of the spaghetti! Now, isn't that a brilliant idea?"

Before Nicky had a chance to reply, Olive returned. Fortunately, John could not see out of the spaghetti tangle, so he was unable to watch them raise the large can over his head and begin to pour. He realized what was going on only when he felt the cold, slippery oil slithering its way all over him.

"Now!" shouted Mr. Pipelli. "Wriggle!"

John did as he was told and, after a few minutes of wriggling and hopping, he felt himself begin to slip out of the tangle. With a final shiver and shake, he popped out and was free. All the spaghetti workers gave a cheer of delight.

John was thrilled to be free of the spaghetti. In fact, he was so pleased that he hardly noticed the fact that he was covered not only with little bits of spaghetti but with olive oil too.

Mr. Pipelli beamed with pleasure.

"Now we can try the machine again," he said. "Let's see if we fixed it."

It took only one press of the button. With a great whirring, the machine came back to life, and it worked perfectly.

"We did it!" shouted Mr. Pipelli. "Everybody take a day off!"

The spaghetti workers gave another rousing cheer, and Mr. Pipelli turned to John and Nicky.

"And as for you, my friends," he said, "let's go right to the factory kitchen and have lunch. I asked the chef to cook the best plate of spaghetti he can imagine, so I assure you it should be delicious."

Mr. Pipelli was right. The lunch was even tastier than the one that John and Nicky had eaten in the restaurant. There was not just one plate of spaghetti for each person—there were six! There was:

For the first course, spaghetti with special cheese sauce, made out of Swiss cheese with holes. The spaghetti was threaded through the holes of the cheese and tied in bows!

For the second course, a single strand of spaghetti ten yards long. This strand was curled around and around on the plate and had to be sucked up and swallowed all in one bite!

For the third course, spaghetti that was plain on the outside but that had the sauce inside the hollow center. Many have tried to make such spaghetti, but only Mr. Pipelli could do it.

For the fourth course, Indian cobra spaghetti. This spaghetti stood up like a cobra.

It swayed as you tried to eat it, but it was very delicious when caught.

For the fifth course, needle spaghetti. This spaghetti was so thin that you could suck it into your mouth through the spaces between your teeth!

For the sixth, and final, course, ordinary spaghetti in the most delicious tomato sauce imaginable. There was oodles of sauce, which had to be slurped up with the spaghetti. Everybody made a lot of noise doing this and got covered with sauce, more or less from head to toe. Second helpings were served—twice!

Afterward, as full and as happy as they had ever been in their lives, the children were led by Mr. Pipelli to the front door and ushered into a waiting car.

"Thank you so much for all your help," he said as he shook hands with both of them. "And perhaps we will meet again one day. After all, who knows what life can bring?"

The car pulled away from the factory, with Mr. Pipelli still standing on the steps waving to his departing guests. Inside the car, John and Nicky were happier than they had been for years. It didn't matter that John had a blob of spaghetti dough lodged down the back of his shirt. It didn't matter that the rest of his clothes were covered with sticky strands of spaghetti, as well as soaked in olive oil. And it didn't matter that Nicky's dress was splattered with hundreds of reminders of the tomato sauce. It had been a marvelous, exciting day and they both knew they would remember every second of it forever.

Aunt Rebecca
Gets to Work

"Look at you!" yelled Aunt Rebecca, quivering with rage. "Just look at you!"

John hung his head. He had to admit that he looked a bit unsightly, covered with spaghetti and all, but wouldn't it all wash off easily enough?

"And as for you, Nicky," Aunt Rebecca continued. "What were you doing letting your brother become such a mess? And look at your dress—ruined!"

"I was holding a flashlight!" Nicky said timidly. "Mr. Pipelli had John on his shoulders, and—"

"On his *what?*" cried Aunt Rebecca. "You both obviously have a lot of explaining to do!"

John tried to tell his aunt about what happened, but it only seemed to make matters worse. At the end of his explanation, her face was stormy with anger.

"I should have known that something like this would happen," she said. "Nothing good could be expected to come from a spaghetti factory! And as for that Mr. Pipelli, I hope that he has a good explanation when I see him tomorrow."

"You're seeing him tomorrow?" Nicky asked. "Why?"

"To complain," snapped Aunt Rebecca. "Do you think I'm going to let him get away with all of this?"

John and Nicky were silent. When Aunt Rebecca made up her mind about something, they knew there was nothing they could do to persuade her otherwise.

The next day Aunt Rebecca told John and Nicky to get ready to go with her to Mr. Pipelli's factory. They were very unwilling to go, since the last thing they wanted to do was to complain to the generous and likable Mr. Pipelli, but their aunt insisted.

They arrived at the factory in sunken spirits.

"It's going to be awful," Nicky whispered to John. "She's going to make a terrible scene."

"I know," John said under his breath. "And Mr. Pipelli will think that we put her up to it."

The man at the factory gate tried to tell Aunt Rebecca that it would be impossible for her to see Mr. Pipelli, but she brushed him off.

"If you don't show me to his office," she said, "then I will find my own way there."

The man looked Aunt Rebecca up and down and decided that she was not a person to be trifled with. Reluctantly, he led the three of them to the door marked The Boss.

Aunt Rebecca knocked once but did not wait for an answer. Throwing the door wide open, she burst into Mr. Pipelli's room and marched up to the astonished spaghetti manufacturer's desk. Mr. Pipelli sprang to his feet and, hiding his surprise, bowed to Aunt Rebecca.

"My dear lady," he said, reaching for her

hand. "How kind of you to visit me. I take it that you're the aunt of my two friends."

Aunt Rebecca stopped in her tracks.

"Please," said Mr. Pipelli, kissing her hand. "Please allow me to offer you a chair."

By now, Aunt Rebecca, overcome by the politeness and charm of the famous spaghetti manufacturer, was completely incapable of complaining.

"Actually," she began, "I was very . . . um . . . very angry . . ."

She stopped. Mr. Pipelli had seated her in a chair and had offered her a peppermint from a silver bowl on his desk.

"I don't eat candy," said Aunt Rebecca.

"How wise!" said Mr. Pipelli. "If only other people were as smart as you."

Aunt Rebecca looked suspiciously at Mr. Pipelli.

"I don't see how you can say that," she said. "After all, you make all that spaghetti that people cover with tomato sauce and terrible things like that."

Mr. Pipelli waved his hand in the air.

"Well, maybe you could help me," he said,

smiling in a charming way. "I've always wanted to make a healthier spaghetti, but I've never found the right recipe."

For the first time that day, Aunt Rebecca smiled.

"Maybe I could help," she said, warming to his idea. "Maybe I could invent . . . carrot-flavored spaghetti!"

Mr. Pipelli clapped his hands.

"My dear lady," he said. "What a brilliant idea! Please, please, do that for me. I would be so grateful if you did." And at that, Mr. Pipelli rose to his feet and kissed her hand again, making Aunt Rebecca look down at the floor and blush.

Aunt Rebecca was silent on the way back home. When they reached the house, the two children watched her as she went straight to the kitchen and closed the door behind her.

"She really means it," said Nicky. "She's really going to invent carrot-flavored spaghetti."

"It'll taste awful," said John. "The only people who will even think about eating it will be the members of the Carrot and Nut League."

Aunt Rebecca remained in the kitchen for the rest of the day. She came out briefly at lunchtime to hand the children a plate of lettuce sandwiches to eat, but she seemed too preoccupied to talk.

At four o'clock in the afternoon, John began to worry. He knocked on the door and asked her if she was all right, but he received no more than a grunt in reply. At five o'clock he knocked again, and this time Aunt Rebecca opened the door and peered out at him.

"Yes," she said. "What is it?"

"I was wondering if you were okay," John said. "We haven't seen you all day."

Aunt Rebecca dried her hands on her apron.

"I'm perfectly fine," she said. "And dinner will be at the normal time—seven on the dot." Then she closed the door.

Mr. Pipelli
Comes to Lunch

John and Nicky were sitting at the table at five minutes to seven. At seven o'clock exactly, the kitchen door opened and Aunt Rebecca came out carrying a large bowl with a small cloud of steam rising from it. It was obvious to the children that this was not a dish of raw onions or carrot soup. But what was it?

"Spaghetti," announced Aunt Rebecca simply. "You keep telling me how much you like the stuff, so I've made you some."

Nicky's mouth fell open in surprise. "Spaghetti?" she exclaimed. "Real spaghetti?"

"Yes," Aunt Rebecca said proudly. "Even better, this is the first bowl—the very first bowl—of carrot-flavored spaghetti. I just invented it, and I will introduce that Pipelli man to it tomorrow."

John and Nicky watched suspiciously as the newly invented spaghetti was ladled onto their plates. It looked like ordinary spaghetti in shape, but it was undeniably carrot-colored.

"Eat up," said Aunt Rebecca. "It won't taste nearly as good if you let it get cold."

Reluctantly, John and Nicky wound the yellow strands around their forks and then put them into their mouths. They looked down at their plates, and then at each other.

"Well?" asked Aunt Rebecca. "What do you think?"

"It's marvelous," said John.

"Wonderful!" said Nicky.

And they meant it. Aunt Rebecca had invented the most delicious spaghetti they'd ever tasted. It was a miracle, and they were right there in the house when it had happened! Without stopping, they finished the rest of the spaghetti and then passed the empty plates to their aunt for more.

"My word!" exclaimed Aunt Rebecca, her face breaking out into a contented smile.

"That's the first time you've asked for more—ever!"

Aunt Rebecca called Mr. Pipelli the next morning, and invited him to the house for lunch. He agreed to come, and when he arrived at the front door he had presents for everyone. John and Nicky each received a fountain pen with a real gold point, and for Aunt Rebecca there was a bouquet of red roses. She became completely speechless when he gave them to her, and when he bent and kissed her hand again, the children noticed that she blushed so much that she made the roses look pale.

The new spaghetti was served for lunch. Everyone eagerly awaited Mr. Pipelli's reaction, and when it came they were not disappointed. As he took the first mouthful, his eyes rolled up to the ceiling in ecstasy. Then, on the second mouthful, he threw his hands up, leaped to his feet, and tossed his napkin out of the window in his excitement.

"It is magnificent!" he said, when he had recovered enough to speak. "We will start manufacturing this spaghetti immediately."

He sat down and looked seriously at Aunt Rebecca.

"You have done the world of spaghetti-making a great service," he said solemnly. "And that will never be forgotten. Never!"

"What a nice man you are," said Aunt Rebecca. "For a spaghetti manufacturer," she added. "Would you like to join us for lunch tomorrow?"

Mr. Pipelli nodded his head enthusiastically, and said that this would give him the greatest pleasure. John thought that he should warn him that lunch could be raw onions and seaweed, but he did not get the opportunity to speak to him privately.

John didn't need to worry. Mr. Pipelli sat at the table the following day and ate his raw onions with every appearance of enjoyment. At the end, to the astonishment of the two children, he asked for more.

"Delicious," Mr Pipelli said, smacking his lips loudly. "And so very good for the system!"

"Absolutely," said Aunt Rebecca, as she ladled more onions onto her visitor's plate.

Mr. Pipelli came back to lunch the next day,

and the day after that. He and Aunt Rebecca seemed to get along very well, and they always took a walk around the neighborhood after the meal. Mr. Pipelli would pick roses from Aunt Rebecca's rosebushes (something she normally never allowed anybody to do), and would present them to her with a low bow.

Finally, exactly one week later, Mr. Pipelli announced that he had asked Aunt Rebecca to marry him and that she had accepted. They would be married the following Saturday, and would all move into his mansion near the spaghetti factory.

"Your charming aunt will become Mrs. Pipelli," he said proudly. "And you, my dear children, will become my stepnephew and stepniece. You can stay with us until your parents have found all the volcanoes they can. After all, there can't be that many. That is, of course, if you agree to this little change in your lives."

"Of course we do," shouted Nicky, and she kissed Aunt Rebecca on the cheek.

Aunt Rebecca smiled. She seemed much less severe now—it was almost as if she had caught Mr. Pipelli's habit of beaming with pleasure at everything he saw.

Because Aunt Rebecca was in such a good mood, later that day John decided to ask her about the last time she had been engaged to be married.

"It was a very long time ago," she explained. "He was a pastry chef, you know—a very good one. He was a kind man, too."

"Then what happened?" asked John. "Did he run away?"

For a moment or two Aunt Rebecca looked sorrowful again, as if she were remembering something very sad.

"No," she said. "He didn't run away. It's just that he was a bit . . . greedy. In fact, he was terribly, terribly greedy. When we ate meals together, he would take things from my plate and pop them into his mouth. I don't think he even knew he was doing it."

She paused, dabbing at a tear that had appeared in the corner of her eye.

"He made our wedding cake himself," she said. "It was the most beautiful cake you can imagine. It was covered with at least four bowls of marzipan and there were six tiers of white icing. Then, the day before the wedding, when I knew that the cake would be finished, I went to look at it. And that's when I changed my mind."

John wondered what Aunt Rebecca could possibly have seen to make her call off the wedding.

"There he was," she said. "He was sitting in his kitchen, looking very pleased with himself. And do you know what he had done? *He had eaten the cake—every last crumb of it!*"

"All six tiers?" asked Nicky, astonished that one person could be so greedy as to eat his own wedding cake—before the wedding.

"Yes," said Aunt Rebecca grimly. "And when he saw me, he looked very guilty. So I said to him, Octavius Hunt (that was what his name was), you will have to find somebody else to marry you, I'm afraid! You are way, way too greedy for me!"

"Mr. Pipelli would never do anything like that," said John.

At the mention of Mr. Pipelli's name, Aunt Rebecca cheered up.

"Of course he wouldn't," she said, closing her eyes dreamily. "What a marvelous man he is!"

From that day on, Aunt Rebecca was a different person. She never scowled, she was cheerful all day, and everything about her seemed so much brighter. But, most remarkable of all, was the change that occurred in Aunt Rebecca's views on food. Of course, John and Nicky didn't expect her to give up all her ideas—and she still believed in the beneficial effect of carrots and onions—but she did seem to be a little more prepared to accept that there was nothing really wrong with spaghetti, even if you put some thick sauce on it. And that, as far as John and Nicky were concerned, was a major breakthrough.

The day before the wedding, Aunt Rebecca went so far as to cook them some of the ordinary spaghetti that Mr. Pipelli had given her. She tasted it herself, and she had to admit that it was delicious, even if it wasn't as delicious as her own carrot-flavored variety.

"I suppose I should eat this from now on," she said, a little bit hesitantly. "After all, starting tomorrow I will be the new Mrs. Pipelli, and I will have responsibilities toward the spaghetti industry."

John tried not to catch Nicky's eye. If he did, he knew that it would be difficult not to smile.

The wedding was a splendid event. Aunt Rebecca carried a bouquet of yellow flowers that Nicky had picked especially for her from the garden of Mr. Pipelli's mansion, and Mr. Pipelli beamed more than you would have thought it possible for anybody to beam. Outside, there were crowds of spaghetti workers who cheered heartily as the happy couple emerged.

"Hooray!" they shouted in unison. "And may you be happy for the rest of your lives."

"Thank you, all," responded Mr. Pipelli. "And take one week's extra vacation, starting today."

This led to an even bigger commotion,

which brought the traffic to a standstill and made people for miles around open their windows to see what great event was happening.

John and Nicky watched all this, their hearts full of happiness. Then, as a large car pulled up to take Mr. Pipelli and Aunt Rebecca to their honeymoon in Italy, John and Nicky joined the happy spaghetti workers throwing confetti at the newlyweds.

But it was not confetti they threw—it was spaghetti—which is an unusual thing to throw at a wedding. But on this occasion, it was just right.

The
Doughnut Ring

Contents

Jim Has an Idea

Jim and his friends were all shocked when they heard the news. They liked Mr. Pride, the school janitor, and the story of what had happened to him was very sad.

"If I could find the person who stole his car," said Jim, "I'd . . . I'd—"

"Steal it back for him?" interrupted Katie.

"Yes," said Jim. "Except it wouldn't be stealing, would it? It would just be taking back what always belonged to Mr. Pride."

Everybody agreed. Mr. Pride had been very attached to his car, although it was incredibly old and made a dreadful noise. It was a battered old vehicle, half blue and half white, with wheels that looked a little wobbly.

But Mr. Pride said it was the best car he had ever owned, and he would never be able to find one just like it.

"Can't you buy another one?" asked Jim, as he and his friends stood around Mr. Pride in the schoolyard.

The janitor shook his head.

"I don't think I can afford it," he said. "I'm going to be retiring soon, and I'm saving my money. I just won't have the cash."

The more Jim thought about it, the more unfair it seemed. He hoped that the police would be able to find the car and get it back for Mr. Pride, but apparently there was not much of a chance of that. So Mr. Pride would have to do without a car and give up the Saturday afternoon trips to the country that he had always enjoyed so much.

Then, without knowing exactly where it came from, Jim had an idea. It was one of those ideas that are so brilliant and so exciting that they have to be announced immediately. Jim did not waste any time. He called together his two best friends, Katie and Mark, and told them what he had in mind.

"Do you think we could do it?" Mark asked hesitantly. "It's a lot of money."

Jim nodded. "You can do anything if you really want to," he said, not completely sure whether to believe this himself.

"Well," said Katie, sounding doubtful. "It's one thing to say you're going to organize a bake sale outside the school each Saturday morning, but what are you going to sell?"

Jim had not thought of that yet, and so he mentioned the first thing that came to his mind.

"Doughnuts," he said simply. "Yes, doughnuts! Everybody likes doughnuts."

That afternoon, the three of them went to the principal, Mrs. Craddock, and told her about their plan. She listened carefully, and then, at the end, she smiled.

"It's a very, very kind idea," she said. "And I'm sure that Mr. Pride would be very touched by it. But do you really think it would work?"

Jim nodded. "We could at least try it," he said enthusiastically. "If people knew that the bake sale was to raise money for a car for

Mr. Pride, then they'd all come. I know they would."

Mrs. Craddock nodded. "He's very popular, isn't he? Yes, I'm sure they'd come."

She thought for a while. Jim was worried that the answer would be no, but then suddenly, she smiled.

"Why not?" she said. "You can try it for one or two Saturdays, and if it works then you can continue." She paused. "But if it doesn't work, then that will have to be the end of it. Do you agree?"

All three of them nodded vigorously.

"Thank you," said Jim. "I'll put up a flyer and we can have the first one this Saturday."

Jim, Mark, and Katie began to make their plans. None of them actually knew how to make doughnuts, but Jim said that his mother had a recipe. When he told her why they wanted to make the doughnuts, she was very pleased. She liked Mr. Pride too. She said that the three children could make the doughnuts that Friday in her kitchen, and that she would be happy to do the frying.

It was a lot of fun getting ready. All the in-gredients were measured out carefully, the trays were dusted with flour (Jim did that), and the mixing bowls and spoons were lined up, ready for use.

Katie read out the recipe, telling people what to do. Mark did the mixing (until his arms got tired and Katie took over), and Jim molded the batter into doughnut shapes. Then, when they were finished carefully lay-ing out the batter on trays, Mark's mother be-gan to fry the doughnuts.

The smell itself was delicious. There's nothing like a doughnut smell to get the taste buds working, and by the time they took the doughnuts out of the pan, all three of them could hardly wait to sink their teeth into one.

They had to wait until they were cool, though. Then they all dusted them with sugar, and Jim took out one doughnut for testing. He cut it into three equal pieces, and then, all at the same time, they popped the doughnut pieces into their mouths and began to chew.

Delicious! Jim had hardly dared to hope that the doughnuts would taste as good as the ones that you could buy at the store, but these did. In fact, they tasted even better.

"Everybody is going to love these," said Katie. "They're going to sell like . . ."

". . . like hotcakes," finished Mark.

Jim agreed. He had been worried about the success of his great idea, but now he was certain. It was going to work!

Doughnuts for Sale

That Saturday Jim, Katie, and Mark were in front of the school just on time. Jim set up the table, and Katie and Mark laid the doughnuts on the tablecloth. They had prepared several signs, all saying BIG DOUGHNUT SALE and explaining the purpose of the sale. These were displayed in places where people would be sure to spot them.

The school was near some stores, and so there were always lots of people passing by on a Saturday morning. As Jim and his friends stood behind the table, the doughnuts laid out temptingly before them, the first of the morning shoppers appeared.

"Those look good," said a woman with a red hat. "Can I try one?"

She picked up a doughnut and took a bite from the edge.

"Mmm," she said. "That's a good doughnut."

She bought four. Then, a few minutes later, two children walked by and stopped to sniff the doughnuts. They did not have a lot of money, but they were able to buy one between the two of them, which they split then and there and ate right away.

"Very good," they said, as they licked the sugar off their fingers.

Now more people arrived. Everybody seemed eager to buy a doughnut, and it was difficult to keep up with the demand. In fact, after only ten minutes had gone by, they realized that they were going to run out of doughnuts. They had proved to be very popular.

Finally, the last two doughnuts were sold, and the sale came to an end. It had taken exactly fifteen minutes to sell every single doughnut.

Jim began to count the money. It added up

to a good sum, and he tucked it safely into the pocket of his jacket. It would take a very long time to save up enough money to buy Mr. Pride a car, since even an old car would cost a lot, but at least this was a good start. Even if it took a year, he would still be able to have the car by the time he retired.

Jim had just finished counting the money and was helping to pack away the table and the tablecloth when the trouble began. People who had heard of the doughnut sale were still arriving, and as they arrived they asked where the doughnuts were.

"I'm sorry," said Katie. "They're all sold out."

"But we've come all this way and we expected doughnuts," said a disappointed voice. "You can't let us down."

"But they're all gone," explained Katie. "They were so good that everybody bought more than one."

"Yes," said Jim, coming to Katie's defense. "It's not our fault."

"Yes, it is," one shopper called out angrily. "You should have had enough doughnuts to go around."

"I'm going to complain to the principal," somebody in the back said. "You just wasted everybody's time."

Jim looked around helplessly. He thought it was unfair that they were being blamed for the fact that the doughnuts sold out. And if somebody complained to Mrs. Craddock, then they probably would not be allowed to have the sale again.

And it soon looked as if he was right.

That Monday morning, Mrs. Craddock called him into her office. She looked angry, and Jim's heart sank at the thought of what she might say.

"There's been a complaint," she began. "In fact, there have been two complaints—from very angry people."

Jim hung his head.

"I'm sorry," he said. "All the doughnuts sold out so quickly. We had no idea it would only take fifteen minutes."

Mrs. Craddock nodded.

"I understand that, Jim," she said. "I know it wasn't your fault. But the problem is that if you don't have enough doughnuts, then you're going to have disappointed people. And you know how people are—they'll blame the school for something like that, even though it's nobody's fault."

Jim realized that what she said was right. But he was very unwilling to give up his idea.

"Give us another chance," he pleaded. "We'll get more doughnuts for next Saturday. Please."

"But how are you going to do that?" asked Mrs. Craddock. "Surely the three of you won't have the time to make that many?"

Jim racked his brain for a solution. Once again, one of his brilliant ideas seemed to float into his head.

"We'll get other people to make some too," he said. "We'll have enough. I promise."

Mrs. Craddock thought for a minute. Then she said, "One more chance, then. We'll see how things go next Saturday morning."

Jim thanked her and went off to tell the good news to Katie and Mark.

"That's nice," said Katie. "But who's going to make more doughnuts? You tell me that!"

Of course Jim had no answer. He thought

about it all that day, and he thought about it the next morning too. He asked some of his other friends if they would make doughnuts for him, but they shook their heads and said no. It wasn't that they didn't want to help Mr. Pride, it's just that making doughnuts was difficult, and something they thought they probably couldn't do.

As he walked home that afternoon, Jim thought that he would probably have to go to Mrs. Craddock and tell her that they would cancel the next sale. He had promised her that there would be enough doughnuts, but he now thought that it was very unlikely that he would be able to keep his promise.

Then, he stopped in his tracks. He had had another brilliant idea! This time, it was even more brilliant than his other ideas.

"Yes," he said to himself. "What a marvelous idea!"

Turning around, he raced over to Katie's house.

Katie had not been expecting him. She set aside her homework and listened to Jim as he explained his idea to her.

"An e-mail chain?" she said. "What's that?"

"Well," said Jim. "I've never actually started one, but what people do is write to somebody else and ask them to write to another person. And then these people each write to more people, and so it goes. Eventually hundreds and hundreds of people end up writing e-mails."

"It sounds kind of silly," said Katie. "I don't see the point. And anyway, what does it have to do with doughnuts?"

Jim grinned. Then, his voice lowered, he explained more of his idea.

"We each send an e-mail to one other person and ask them to send us a few doughnuts. That won't be hard. And they won't mind doing it if they know it's for a good cause. Then they each write an e-mail to another person and they ask them to send some doughnuts. And so it goes. Eventually we should have enough doughnuts."

Katie listened to him, her mouth wide open. She had heard Jim come up with some extraordinary ideas before, but this one was surely the most extraordinary.

"But . . . ," she said. "But . . ."

"Please," said Jim. "Please, let's try. It can't hurt."

Katie was not convinced. She wasn't sure e-mail chains were a good idea.

"Well," she said, after a while, "we could try, I guess."

"Good," said Jim. "Now, where's your computer? We should get these e-mails sent right away."

Waiting for the Mail

It did not take long to write the e-mails. Katie had an aunt who was a very good cook; she wrote to her. Jim wrote to a friend of his mother's, who lived on the other side of town, and then he wrote to his older cousin as well. He wasn't sure whether the cousin would help, but there was always a chance.

Our school janitor's car has been stolen, the e-mails said. *We are trying to raise money to help him buy another one, and so we are having a doughnut sale every Saturday. Please could you help us by making some doughnuts and bringing them to us as soon as you can? If you can't bring them, you can send them through the mail. Then, could you write to another person who you think might help and ask them to do the same?*

"I hope it works!" Jim said to himself as he sent off the e-mails.

The e-mails were sent on Tuesday. It was too early for anything to happen on Wednesday, but by Thursday morning Jim was already beginning to worry. When he came home from school that day, he asked his mother whether anything had been delivered for him, but she shook her head.

"What are you expecting?" she asked inquisitively.

"Oh, just a few doughnuts," Jim replied.

Then he told her about the plan. She looked very doubtful.

"It won't work," she said. "Chain e-mails never work. People never pay attention to them."

"I know that," said Jim. "But this one is for a very good cause."

"We'll see," said his mother. "In the meantime, we had better make some doughnuts for Saturday. You can't rely on any doughnuts appearing out of thin air!"

So Jim and his mother made the same

amount of doughnuts that they had all made the previous week. The doughnuts looked and smelled every bit as delicious as the previous ones had, but Jim knew that there would never be enough to satisfy everybody who turned up at the sale.

Friday morning came, and Jim anxiously awaited the arrival of the mailman.

"Any packages for me?" he inquired as the mailman brought the mail to the front door.

"Sorry," said the mailman, looking at a list. "Nothing here for you. What are you waiting for?"

"Doughnuts," said Jim sadly. "Lots and lots of doughnuts."

The mailman laughed. "Just the sort of package I like to deliver," he joked. "Well, I hope they arrive soon!"

At school that day, Jim told Katie and Mark the bad news. The other two had not expected to receive anything, since the e-mails had all given Jim's address. They were both very disappointed.

"Tomorrow will be the last sale," said Mark.

"There'll be the same kind of trouble and Mrs. Craddock will be furious."

"I know," said Jim dejectedly.

"There's always tomorrow," said Katie. "Remember that people haven't had much time."

Jim would have liked to agree, but he now had no hope that any doughnuts would arrive before it was time to start the sale.

"Maybe we should cancel it now," Mark suggested. "We could put up a sign at the front of the school. That might be the best thing to do."

Both Jim and Katie thought that this was not a good idea. They would go ahead, they said, even if it involved facing more disappointed customers. At least some people would get the doughnuts they wanted, which, after all, was better than nothing.

The next morning, Jim did not even think about the mailman. So he was very surprised when the doorbell rang and his mother answered the door.

"Jim!" she called from the hall. "Package for you. Or should I say, packages!"

Jim rushed out of his room to see the mailman standing in the doorway with two large boxes in his arms.

"These are the most delicious-smelling packages I've delivered for a very long time," he said, smiling widely. "Doughnuts, I'd guess!"

Jim took the boxes gratefully and rushed with them to the kitchen. He gently unwrapped them and took out the plastic bags that were inside. Within the bags, carefully wrapped in greaseproof paper, were doughnuts—dozens of them.

He laid the doughnuts on a tray. They were marvelous. Some had jelly in them, some had almond custard. Some were plain. But they all—every single one of them—looked delicious!

When Katie and Mark arrived at Jim's house, expecting to have to carry only those doughnuts that Jim and his mother had made, they were astonished to see the array that was set out on the kitchen table.

"But there are hundreds," said Katie. "Look at all of them!"

"Yes," said Jim. "Half of them were made by your aunt, and half by my mother's friend."

"There will definitely be enough for everyone now," said Mark, who was itching to try one of the doughnuts himself. "In fact, there'll be too many."

He reached out to pick up a particularly mouthwatering doughnut, but Jim caught him by the wrist before he could touch it.

"No," he said. "We asked people to make them for Mr. Pride, not for us."

"If there are any left over, you can eat those," said Jim's mother. "Nobody would mind then."

But there weren't any left over. Again, the sale was well-attended, and there was a large crowd gathered in front of the school, but the number of doughnuts on sale was exactly right, and at the end of the sale there was not a single one left.

Jim glowed with pride as he told his mother about how well the sale had gone and how none of the customers had gone away empty-handed.

"I'm very glad to hear it," she said. "Because while you were away, something arrived for you. It's in the kitchen."

Jim was curious to see what it was. He went straight to the kitchen and looked inside. There, on the table, was a large box. Just by sniffing, Jim was able to tell what it contained.

Doughnuts!

The Doughnut Deluge

The doughnuts had come from Jim's older cousin, who had dropped them at the house himself. On top of the box was a note.

Dear Jim, it read. *I'm very happy to help you with your doughnut sale. Here are some that I have baked myself. I also wrote to two friends, who I am sure will help you. Good luck!*

Jim was delighted. These doughnuts could be put in the fridge and kept until next Saturday's sale. Together with the next batch that he and his mother would make, there would be enough for that week. With his mother's help, he stored all the doughnuts away, taking only the tiniest crumb of one to taste for himself. It was superb!

That afternoon, there was a knock on the door. Jim answered it to find a delivery man standing outside, holding a box.

"Is your name Jim Hargreaves?" he asked in a businesslike voice.

"Yes," said Jim, eyeing the box. He had a good idea what it contained.

"Delivery for you," said the man. "Please sign here."

Jim signed the receipt and took the box into the kitchen. This time the doughnuts were from somebody he did not know at all. It was one of the people to whom Katie's aunt had written, and it contained three dozen large doughnuts, all dripping with red jelly.

Jim sighed. It was good to get more dough-nuts, of course, but the fridge was full. These would have to be put in the freezer, and then unfrozen in time for the next sale. So he and his mother popped them all into bags and put them in the freezer.

"I think we'll have some left over next week," said Jim. "Maybe I can give them to people in my class to share with their friends."

"Well, let's hope no more arrive," said Jim's

mother, licking the jelly off her fingers. "We'll have to start putting them in the basement if they do."

No more doughnuts arrived that day, or on the following day, which was Sunday. But on Monday, when Jim returned from school, he knew that something was wrong the second he walked in the door.

"I've had enough of these doughnuts!" his mother called out in an exasperated voice. "Another six batches arrived today. *Six!* This is really going to have to stop."

Jim made his way down to the basement to see the new doughnuts. They had come from all kinds of people—some delivered by hand, and others through the mail. Everybody had written a note, saying how they had not broken the chain and had written to more of their friends to ask them to join in. They were all sure that the friends would be happy to help.

Jim did not know what to do. When he had started the e-mail chain, he had no idea that it would be so effective. But now that he thought about it, he realized that an enormous number of doughnuts could result if everybody got other people to make a batch. It was like a picture of a tree, with roots spreading out below, more numerous and widespread the further away one got from the top. And what would the end be? A thousand doughnuts? Several thousand? Even more?

Jim swallowed hard. Where would he even begin to put a million doughnuts? He had no idea.

By the time Saturday arrived, you could smell the doughnuts all through the house. Katie and Mark had helped make more posters, which they hoped would attract more people to the sale, but even if many more people came this week, could they possibly hope to sell all the doughnuts that had arrived, and were still arriving?

On Saturday morning, they started to take the doughnuts to the sale very early. They put out extra tables, but even with these, there was not enough room to display them all. And when people came to buy, they were given not only the number they asked for, but six free

ones as well. Everybody was delighted with this, and some people even had the nerve to ask whether they could get their six free ones without buying any doughnuts in the first place.

At the end of the morning, when they had served their last customer, the exhausted three looked into the last of the boxes to see what was left. There, inside, sticking to the bottom of the box, were three large and succulent-looking doughnuts. They each took one and ate it hungrily. Then, when everything was cleaned up, they all went home.

"I don't want to see another doughnut for at least a week," Mark said. "I'm sick of them."

"So am I," said Katie. "I'll probably dream about them tonight."

Jim said nothing. He was worried about what he might see when he got home.

And he had good reason to worry. Because there, in front of the house, were the morning's deliveries.

More doughnuts!

Katie Has an Idea

Jim's mother was sitting in the kitchen with her head in her hands.

"We're going to have to do something about all these doughnuts," she said. "We can't take any more. I knew this e-mail chain would get out of hand. You're going to have to write to people and ask them not to send any more."

Jim scratched his head.

"I wish I could," he said. "But I don't know who to write to. The e-mails have been sent all over the place by now. I could never find out where they went."

"But we just can't take more doughnuts," wailed his mother. "Where are we going to put them? I had to put ten boxes in the basement this morning. There are doughnuts in my bedroom and doughnuts under your bed. And that's just from today's deliveries. What on earth is going to happen when more arrive next week?"

Jim could not answer this question. "I will have to have another brilliant idea," he told himself. But the trouble with his brilliant ideas was that they did not always come when they were needed.

On Monday, when the mailman brought more doughnuts to the front door, Jim asked him to take them back.

"I can't do that," the mailman said, shaking his head. "That's against our policy. Once a package is sent to you, you have to take it."

Reluctantly, Jim took the packages and stacked them in the kitchen. As he stood over them, wondering what to do, a brilliant idea came into his head. He would give the doughnuts away! All he had to do was put a sign outside the house saying FREE DOUGHNUTS! INQUIRE WITHIN! All the neighbors could help themselves.

So the sign went up, and the neighbors did take advantage of the offer. Some brought large bags and took away dozens at a time. Others were less greedy but still took a few.

At the end of the day, hundreds of dough-nuts had been given away. The following day, though, fewer people came by for their free doughnuts. Everybody had enough to last them for some time. Unfortunately, on that very day there were twenty more deliveries of doughnuts as the e-mail chain was sent to more and more people. This meant that even after giving away so many doughnuts, they were left with as many as they had in the first place. There seemed to be no escape!

Jim discussed the problem with Katie and Mark.

"We bit off more than we can chew here," he said. "Our house is full of doughnuts, and they keep coming."

Katie and Mark were silent. They could think of nothing to say, and although they were sorry for Jim, they were both secretly relieved that the doughnuts were going to his house and not to theirs.

Then Katie came up with an idea. "If we can't sell these doughnuts," she said, "then maybe somebody else could."

Jim looked at her blankly. "But we tried giving them away," he said. "We have too many, even to do that. There's nobody left in this town who wants any more doughnuts."

"There might be somebody," said Katie. "Can you think of who it could be?"

Jim frowned. Who could possibly want to take thousands of doughnuts? Then it dawned on him.

"Do you mean Mr. Windram?" he burst out.

"Yes," said Katie, smiling. "Mr. Wallace Windram, the supermarket king. If anybody can take the doughnuts off our hands, it'll be him."

Katie's idea was certainly a promising one. Mr. Wallace Windram was the most well-known and richest person for miles around. He lived in a large house at the edge of town, and from there he managed the great business that he had built up single-handedly. Throughout the country you could see his supermarkets— massive, barnlike buildings, filled to the brim with tasty food.

"If he agrees to take our doughnuts and sell them in his shops, our problem will be solved," said Jim. "What a marvelous idea!"

Katie blushed. Everybody was so used to Jim having brilliant ideas, so it was nice to have one herself—just for a change! And anyway, look where his brilliant ideas had landed them—in the middle of a mountain of doughnuts, that's where!

Mr. Windram, Supermarket King

Everybody knew where Mr. Windram lived, but it seemed that nobody had ever met him or knew of anybody who had.

"I've seen his picture in the newspapers," said Mark. "He's usually opening things or presenting prizes."

"I know," said Katie. "But how can we actually get to see him?"

"Call him," said Jim, in the voice that he used to express his brilliant ideas.

"But will he be in the phone book?" asked Mark. "Very important people sometimes don't have their numbers listed."

"We can always look," said Jim, as he went to get a copy of the book.

They looked through the phone book until they reached the place in the Ws where Mr. Windram's name should be. And there it was, with an ordinary number, just like anybody else's. They voted to decide who should make the call, and both Katie and Mark voted for Jim. So, his heart in his mouth, Jim picked up the receiver and dialed the number.

An unfriendly voice answered on the other end. "Mr. Windram's residence," it said.

"Could I speak to Mr. Windram?" asked Jim, trying to make his voice sound as grown-up as he could. But all it did was make him sound as if he had a cold.

"Why do you want to speak to Mr. Windram?" the voice asked icily. "Does he know you?"

"Not exactly," said Jim. "In fact, not at all. It's about . . . er, a business matter."

"Then you can speak to me," cut in the voice. "I handle that kind of thing."

Jim paused. He was sure that this person, whoever he was, would not be the slightest bit interested in doughnuts. And he was right. The unfriendly voice said no, and then repeated his no, and that was it. Jim heard the telephone reverberate as the receiver was slammed down on the other end.

"No luck," he said to the others. "I don't think it's going to be easy to speak to Mr. Windram."

Jim pondered the problem of how he could see Mr. Windram. It was clearly going to be impossible to speak to him on the telephone, and somebody else was sure to open his letters for him. So the only thing to do was to see him in person—if he spoke to him, Jim was sure that he could persuade Mr. Windram to buy all the doughnuts from him. Homemade doughnuts were way more delicious than any doughnuts you could buy at the store. And for some reason, Mr. Windram's stores never sold doughnuts.

There was not a moment to lose. Every day, with every delivery of the mail, more boxes of doughnuts arrived at the house. Jim's mother was becoming desperate. The garbagemen refused to take them, the neighbors couldn't stand the sight of another doughnut, and even a farmer, who was a friend of Jim's mother and had taken some to feed to his pigs, had reported that the pigs were unwilling to eat any more.

"The doughnuts get stuck on their snouts," he said. "They don't like them at all!"

That afternoon, Jim packed a small box of the very best doughnuts he could find. Then, studying a map of the town, he set out for the street where Mr. Windram lived. It was a long bike ride, and he was tired by the time he reached it, but at last he reached the high wall surrounding Mr. Windram's house. Now all he had to do was get inside.

He left his bicycle at the end of the street and began to walk toward Mr. Windram's gate. It was a very impressive gate—tall and ornate—not the kind of gate one could walk up to and open by oneself. As he got closer, Jim saw that something was going on.

Cars were driving up toward the gate and being ushered in by a uniformed butler. It was difficult for Jim to know exactly what was happening, but it seemed as though Mr. Windram was having some kind of party. All the people in the cars were nicely dressed, and faintly, from the other side of the wall, Jim thought he could hear the sounds of a band playing.

Jim's heart sank. He had chosen the worst possible afternoon to try to see Mr. Windram. How could he possibly see him if he was in the middle of holding a large party for all his important friends? His spirits lowered, Jim walked past the gates. He imagined what was happening at home now. More deliveries of doughnuts would be coming, and his poor mother would be frantically searching for somewhere to put them. It was a nightmare.

Then, just as he was about to turn around and head back to his bicycle, Jim saw the branch of a tree. The tree itself was inside Mr. Windram's yard but the branch hung over the wall. Another brilliant idea was about to come!

Crashing the Party

Jim looked over his shoulder. A large car had just driven through the gate, which had swung shut behind it with a clang. Now there was nobody around, and, without waiting, Jim tucked his box of doughnuts under his arm and leaped up and grabbed the hanging branch. For a moment or so his fingers scrabbled for a good grip, but he soon managed a firm hold and succeeded in hauling himself up onto the branch. After that it was a matter of inching slowly forward until he had crossed the top of the wall and could drop down on the other side.

Jim found himself at the very edge of a

long, rolling lawn. In the distance was Mr. Windram's mansion—a great white building with soaring pillars at the front. Along the side of the house, there had been pitched two massive striped tents with open sides. A band was playing in one of the tents and the other was filled with a long table. This was where the party was taking place.

Jim crouched down and ran for the cover of a cluster of bushes. From the safety of his hiding place, he was able to think about what he should do. It was one thing to drop into Mr. Windram's backyard uninvited; it was another thing completely to get to speak to Mr. Windram, wherever he was. Jim imagined that he would be in the second tent, with all of his guests, somewhere at the table. But where?

As Jim was studying the scene, something happened that gave him his chance. One of the waiters who was bringing large silver platters out of the house slipped on something and dropped a tray of desserts all over one of the members of the band. There was a shout and a general kerfuffle as the bandsman stood up and tried to wipe cream and custard off his suit. A large dish of strawberries had fallen into his trombone, and pudding was trickling down his sheets of music.

While everybody's attention was focused on this unfortunate scene, Jim ran forward. Nobody saw him as he darted from bush to bush, nor when he stopped, and hid in a lavender bush right next to the tent. From the bush it was only a lurch and a wiggle to slip under the table.

Underneath the table, there was a forest of legs, all dressed in expensive clothes. Jim squeezed himself past a pair of gold shoes with tiny, sparkling gems. Then, taking care not to touch anybody, he crept over a pair of ankles dressed in bright pink socks and a pair of legs in fancy white silk. Here and there, bits of food had been dropped: a grilled shrimp skewer, half an egg stuffed with caviar, a piece of thin green asparagus on a stick. There were also some very strange things to be seen. He saw an ankle with a large gold watch on it (how on Earth could they tell the time?). He saw a pair of false teeth that somebody must have dropped and then been too shy to look for. It was all very interesting.

But Jim had not come for the sights. He had come to find Mr. Windram, and he realized that he must be somewhere very close. But which of these legs belonged to Mr. Windram?

Jim studied the legs. All of them looked as if they could belong to a supermarket king. All of them looked like rich legs. Then a thought occurred to him. Surely the host would be sitting at the head of a long table of guests. Mr. Windram was sure to have the best seat, where he could look out at all of his guests, and that must be at the head.

Inch by inch, clutching his precious box of doughnuts to his chest, Jim crawled up toward the head of the table. When he eventually reached it, he stopped. There were six legs there, which all looked roughly the same. There were three people seated at the head, and any one of them could be Mr. Windram.

For a few minutes, Jim had no idea what to do. If he spoke to the wrong set of legs, then

he would be discovered and thrown out before he had the chance to plead his case to Mr. Windram. So he had to choose the right legs.

Jim edged forward again until he was only a few inches away from the legs. He stared hard at them, trying to decide which pair of shoes looked more expensive than the others. But the shoes all looked pretty much the same.

Then Jim noticed the tag. One of the socks on one of the legs was showing a tag. Jim stretched his neck forward and scrunched up his eyes to see what the tag said. *Wind* . . . the legs moved, and Jim had to crane his neck to read the tag again. *Wind* . . . Yes! *Windram's Famous Striped Socks*, the tag said. Jim had heard of them. They were sold at bargain prices near the counters of every Windram's supermarket. No rich person would wear such cheap socks unless he was the person who made them in the first place. Jim knew then that he was looking at the legs of the supermarket king!

The Doughnut Deal

Now came the moment of greatest danger. Very carefully, and very quietly, Jim opened his small box of doughnuts. Then, taking the utmost care, he took out the best doughnut available. It was a large one, with a caramel and whipped cream filling, and it would have melted the heart of the sternest person.

With the doughnut held gingerly between his thumb and forefinger, Jim very cautiously pushed aside part of the tablecloth at the side of Mr. Windram's legs. Then, reaching up, he slipped the doughnut up onto the table, leaving it where he thought it would be at the side of Mr. Windram's plate.

Nothing happened. Jim sat still, his heart thumping with excitement. Surely Mr. Windram could not fail to notice it. But there was nothing—not a single sign to suggest that anything unusual was happening. Then, very suddenly, there came a strange noise from above. It was a snort of some kind, and it was followed by a surprised-sounding voice.

"What on Earth is this?" the voice said. "And where did it come from?"

Another voice, belonging to one of the other pairs of legs, replied.

"It looks like a doughnut," this voice said. "I haven't eaten one of those in years."

"Well," said Mr. Windram's voice. "It looks tasty. I might as well try it."

There was silence for a minute. Jim crossed his fingers, praying that it would work. If it didn't, then it would be the end of all his hopes.

"Mmm," said Mr. Windram. "Not bad!"

Then a fist thumped down on the table, making Jim jump.

"Very good!" roared the voice. "Waiter! Another of these . . . doughnut things, please!"

Jim saw a pair of waiter's legs hovering behind Mr. Windram.

"I'm afraid we don't have any, sir," he said timidly. "In fact, I have no idea at all where that one came from."

"Well, it didn't fall out of the sky!" snapped Mr. Windram. "You must have given it to me."

"I'm sorry," said the waiter. "I didn't."

"I wonder who did?" said Mr. Windram.

Listening to this made Jim realize that it was time for him to act. Summoning up all of his courage, he leaned forward and tapped one of Mr. Windram's legs.

"I gave it to you, Mr. Windram," he said. "And I have some more down here!"

After that, everything happened very quickly. There was a big fuss when Jim was discovered under the table, and one of the waiters wanted to throw him out immediately, but he was stopped by Mr. Windram.

"If this young man wants to speak to me,"

said Mr. Windram, "then let him. Come on, young man, what's all this doughnut business? You certainly have delicious doughnuts, if I may say so!"

So Jim sat down next to Mr. Windram and told him the whole story. At the end, when he was telling everyone about how he crawled along under the table, Mr. Windram began to laugh.

"You must have seen some very odd sights down there," he guffawed. "Did you see my brother-in-law's teeth, by the way? He's always losing them at parties."

Jim nodded, which made Mr. Windram laugh even more. Then, wiping the tears of laughter away with a large silk handkerchief, he returned to the serious question of all the doughnuts.

"So you want me to take these doughnuts off your hands and sell them in my supermarkets?" he asked.

"Yes," said Jim. "I'd be very grateful if you could do that."

Mr. Windram narrowed his eyes and stared at Jim.

"And all the money would go to this old janitor . . . Mr. Pride?" he asked.

"Yes," said Jim. "It would."

For a minute or two Mr. Windram said nothing. Then he smiled and patted Jim on the shoulder.

"Do you want to know what I think?" he asked. "I think . . . I think it's a very good idea. Yes, a very good idea indeed. Doughnuts? Let's have lots and lots of doughnuts."

Jim heaved a sigh of relief as Mr. Windram went on to say how he would send some of his men to Jim's house immediately to collect the doughnuts and put them in cold storage.

"Of course, you probably won't get them for much longer," said Mr. Windram. "Sooner or later these e-mail chains stop. But that won't matter. Maybe then you and your mother can make some for me. And I'll pay you well."

"Thank you," he said. "Thank you, Mr. Windram."

Mr. Windram chuckled.

"What about another doughnut?" he said,

pointing to a jelly-filled one that he had spotted in Jim's box. "That one will do."

Mr. Windram ate all the rest of the doughnuts in the box. Then, since the guests were starting to leave, he accompanied Jim to the front gate.

"Come back and see me soon," he said. As Jim hurried down the road, eager to tell Katie and Mark the wonderful news, the supermarket king yelled out to him. "And bring some doughnuts with you!"

"All right," shouted Jim. "I will!"

And Jim did. Mr. Windram liked the doughnuts, of course, and asked for more, which Jim gave to him. Eventually people stopped sending Jim doughnuts, but that didn't really matter. The doughnuts had sold so well in the supermarkets that enough money had been raised to buy Mr. Pride a new car—and a very nice one at that. Jim still saw Mr. Windram, though, since they had become very good friends. Mr. Windram asked Jim whether he would like to come with him on his inspections of his supermarkets, which Jim agreed to do. And after they had finished inspecting a supermarket, they would return to Mr. Windram's house for something to eat.

And what did they have to eat? That's right! Doughnuts.

A Note on the Author

Alexander McCall Smith has written more than fifty books, including the *New York Times* bestselling *No. 1 Ladies' Detective Agency* mysteries and *The Sunday Philosophy Club*. A professor of medical law at Edinburgh University, he was born in what is now Zimbabwe and taught law at the University of Botswana. He lives in Edinburgh, Scotland.

Visit him at www.alexandermccallsmith.com.

A Note on the Illustrator

Laura Rankin is the illustrator of Alexander McCall Smith's Harriet Bean mysteries in addition to the picture books *Ruthie and the (Not So) Teeny Tiny Lie* (which she also wrote), *Rabbit Ears, Swan Harbor*, and *The Handmade Alphabet*. She lives in Maine.

How Do You Make
the Perfect Hamburger?
You Tell Us!

In "The Perfect Hamburger," Joe and Mr. Borthwick make the best hamburger in the world. The recipe calls for meat, onion, rosemary, sage, and . . . well, you'll have to read the story to find out the secret fifth ingredient!

What would be in your perfect hamburger, and how would you cook it?

Send us your original recipe for the perfect hamburger and you could win a book signed by author Alexander McCall Smith, a copy of the popular cookbook *Kids Cook 1-2-3*, an apron, and cooking supplies. Plus, YOUR recipe will be posted on the Bloomsbury USA Web site!

Visit www.bloomsburyusa.com for more information.

BLOOMSBURY
CHILDREN'S
BOOKS

HOW TO ENTER

NO PURCHASE NECESSARY. Contest begins September 1, 2007, and ends December 31, 2007. Enter by printing your name, date of birth, parent's/guardian's name if under the age of 18, full address, and phone number on an 8½" x 11" piece of paper or via e-mail and create your recipe for the perfect hamburger. Mail to: Perfect Hamburger Contest, Bloomsbury Children's Books, 104 Fifth Avenue, New York, NY 10011 or e-mail to children.publicity@bloomsburyusa.com. Entries must be received by Bloomsbury no later than December 31, 2007. Partially completed or illegible entries will not be accepted. Sponsor will not be responsible for lost, late, mutilated, illegible, stolen, incomplete, or misdirected entries, or entries with postage due. All entries become the property of Bloomsbury and will not be returned, so please keep a copy for your records.

ELIGIBILITY

Contest is open to legal residents of the United States and Canada (excluding Quebec, Puerto Rico, Guam, the U.S. Virgin Islands, and where prohibited by law) to persons over eight (8) years of age. All federal, state, and local laws and regulations apply. Void wherever prohibited or restricted by law. Employees (and employees' immediate family and household members) of Sponsor, and its parent, affiliates, subsidiaries, suppliers, printers, distributors, advertising and promotional agencies, and prize suppliers are not eligible to participate in the Contest.

PRIZES

There will be one (1) Grand-Prize Winner selected and two (2) Second-Prize Winners selected. One Grand-Prize Winner will receive a signed copy of *The Perfect Hamburger and Other Delicious Stories*, a copy of *Kids Cook 1-2-3*, an apron, and cooking supplies. Total approximate retail value of Grand Prize: $150.00 U.S. Two (2) Second-Prize Winners will each receive a signed copy of *The Perfect Hamburger and Other Delicious Stories*. Total approximate retail value of Second Prize: $15.95 U.S. No prize substitution except by Sponsor due to unavailability.

WINNERS

All eligible entries received by the end of the contest closing date will be judged by Alexander McCall Smith and the Bloomsbury Marketing Department. All entries submitted in accordance with the submission guidelines contained in these Official Rules will be judged on the basis of creativity, clarity of presentation, and uniqueness of style. Winners will be notified by phone or e-mail on or about January 31, 2008. Any winner notification not responded to or returned as undeliverable may result in prize forfeiture and an alternate winner shall be selected. The potential prize winner and, if the potential prize winner is under the age of 18, the potential prize winner's parent or guardian will be required to sign and return an affidavit of eligibility and release of liability within fourteen (14) days of notification. In the event of noncompliance within this time period or if the prize is returned, refused, or returned as undeliverable, then an additional judging from eligible entries will be made to determine an alternate winner. No substitution or transfer of a prize is permitted except by Sponsor.

RESERVATIONS

By participating, Winner (and if under the age of 18, Winner's parent/legal guardian) agrees that Bloomsbury and its parent companies, assigns, subsidiaries or affiliates, advertising, promotion, fulfillment agencies, and suppliers will have no liability whatsoever, and will be held harmless by Winner (and Winner's parent/legal guardian) for any liability for any injuries, losses, or damages of any kind to person, including death, and property resulting in whole or in part, directly or indirectly, from the acceptance, possession, misuse, or use of the prize, or participation in the contest. By entering the contest, Winner (and if under the age of 18, Winner's parent or legal guardian) consents to the use of Winner's name, likeness, and biographical data for publicity and promotional purposes on behalf of Bloomsbury, with no additional compensation or further permission (except where prohibited by law). For the names of the winners, available after January 31, 2008, please send a stamped, self-addressed envelope to: Bloomsbury Children's Books, Perfect Hamburger Contest Winners, 104 Fifth Avenue, New York, NY 10011.